SUBVERSION

NEON
BOOK ONE

ALLYSON LINDT

ACELETTE PRESS

This book is a work of fiction.

While reference might be made to actual historical events or existing locations, the names, characters, places, and incidents are either the product of the author's imagination or are used fictitiously, and any resemblance to actual persons, living or dead, business establishments, events, or locales is entirely coincidental.

Manufactured in the United States of America
Acelette Press

For my Dahlia

CHAPTER 1

DAHLIA

There weren't a lot of places where a geeky goth girl could say *this feels like home*. Especially one who was raised as an assassin by the gods.

But for me, NEON was one of those spots. After a lifetime of wondering where I belonged, every time I stepped through the deceptively plain doors of the burlesque club, I felt like everything was right in my world.

The tables and bar were wood stained so dark it was black in the dim lighting, neon accentuated the main stage, the curtain, and the bottles on the far wall, and the furnishings were straight out of the 1920's.

The first time I found this place, a few years ago, I swore it was decorated just for me. The perfect eclectic combination of goth meets old-school meets modern tech.

Fenrir—Fen—stood near the entrance as the most imposing bouncer in the whole of history. It wasn't just his physical size, though he was muscled and super sexy in a growly kind of way. It was that he radiated the aura of an ancient god who also happened to be a giant wolf when he wasn't trying to blend in with people.

Seeing him alive was a relief, though. After a series of too-vivid nightmares where I watched him die through a disturbingly first person view, I was grateful to be able to reach out and touch him.

"Hey, handsome," I greeted him with a smile that didn't feel as natural as I wanted. Not his fault —I was just wound tight tonight.

He tugged one of the braids I wore on each side of my head. "Hey, Duckie. You hunting?"

More like hiding. "Not tonight." Not a target. And not a hook-up because I was too high strung to even think about trying to get laid. Habit dictated I turn from him to scan the room a second time and a third, to see what kind of threats waited.

The wolf at my back was the least of my concerns. He was safe. One of the few beings in the world I trusted with my life.

He grabbed my braid again, yanking playfully. "In that case, looking to be hunted? You wore handles and everything."

A whisper of desire flitted through me, muffling my paranoia. Part of my training was seduction, so there was no romantic attachment in the physical relationship I had with Fen and the other bar's owner, Frey. I still knew enough to enjoy the hook-ups when they happened, though.

It was tempting to tilt forward. Let him claim my mouth. Fall into the distraction for the night with a god or two.

The basic reminder erased my creeping lust. Immortals were the problem and the reason I was here. I know a lot more of them than most anyone ever would, including the gods, but I wasn't one of them. I was still a fragile little human.

I shook my head. "I'm just here for the show tonight."

"You know where to find me if you change your mind." He nodded toward a table near the stage.

I doubted I would, but the open-ended offer was nice, and if the show got me worked up, he wouldn't mind distracting me from my problems with a little naked Twister. "Thanks." I headed toward a darker corner near the wall instead of the middle of the room. I wanted to see, not to be seen.

I'd been raised on a campus run by a group of gods who called themselves The Order of Mistletoe. They claimed their existence was to stop a series of ancient prophecies from bringing on Ragnarök. Which sounded noble until one realized they were quite a bit more concerned about the fact that those prophecies had them dying and replaced with other gods, than they were about the end-of-the-world portion of things.

So they'd built an army. Taking mortals with no family from foster homes and out of the system, when we were old enough to understand things like death, but still young enough to be indoctrinated after being lured in by promises of becoming heroes.

Before most of us hit puberty we'd learned the gods were not only real, but that they punished and rewarded immediately, based on our faith and actions.

"Oh my God, Dahlia." A frantic voice drew my gaze from the stage, and a woman sat next to me. Her straight black hair was pulled into long pigtails, framing a pixie-like face. "I can't believe you're here. I'm so glad you are, though. I need your help."

I liked Minato, and at the same time felt a twinge of guilt every time I saw her. She was the reason my partner, Magnus, and I originally came to this club. The elite assassins who came out of TOM were Nobles. Magnus and I weren't their finest—neither of us had top ranks in things like shooting and hand-to-hand combat—but no one was better than us at digital espionage, so we did make the *Noble* list. Minato was a potential god, and we'd been sent to ferret her out and kill her. Obviously we'd failed, and it was a choice on our part.

"What's up?" I'd do a lot of things for Minato that I wouldn't for most people. Not only because of the regret, but that mission helped me walk away from my old life.

"I'm the main show tonight, but my partner called in. I need you to dance with me."

I liked dancing burlesque almost as much as I liked watching it. I was drawn to most visuals that involved sensuality and people embracing their art —men, women, anywhere along the spectrum. In fact, most Nobles were bisexual. A part of our early evaluations, because we had to be willing to seduce —fuck—anyone at any time. Literally or metaphorically.

I'd never been good at the latter, but this time I had to let her down. "I don't know your dance."

"But you do because I learned it from watching you. It's the mirror."

The mirror was a routine Magnus and I did when we were trying to infiltrate the club.

We hadn't realized at the time that we never would've even found NEON if Frey didn't want us to. I still didn't know how he'd realized before me, before he met me, that I didn't want to be a part of TOM anymore. Whenever I asked him his answer was *I just knew.*

"I'll do it if we can wear something to hide my face." I didn't mean to agree, but dancing sounded fun, I got to help Minato, and the whole thing should take my mind off my own woes. "And if you have time to give me a run-down of any changes you've made."

"*Yay.*" Her grin and enthusiasm were contagious. She grabbed my hand and tugged me toward the dressing room in back.

We found an empty space wide enough for her to give me a quick rundown of the routine, which she hadn't made any modifications to.

"It's been a couple of years since you did this. I'm surprised you remember it so well," Minato said.

I shrugged. "Just lucky, I guess." Well, it was a little more than luck. At TOM, most Nobles were exceptional fighters of some sort. Marksmen, hand-to-hand combat, etcetera.

I was okay at those things. My skills were in my brain. Digital espionage to me was like most people getting on Instagram, and I had an accuracy level to my memory that scared most people.

"The costumes are a lot the same too. Really, I pretty much stole your show." She showed me to a rack with clothes hanging from it, and I recognized ours immediately.

Matching black skirts that ruffled out in a flare from the hips to mid-calf, corsets trimmed with violet, long gloves, and top hats. It was steam punk meets goth. "I'm glad someone's getting some use out of it."

The clothing looked intricate. The kind of thing

that should take an hour, and multiple people, to put on. It was all tear away snaps and Velcro, and went on quickly.

I wanted to chat with Minato. Ask her how she'd been. What she was up to. Share the same. It took a lot of restraint for me to bite my tongue and keep the conversation minimal. I tended to ramble when I was nervous or stressed. I'd learned to use that to my advantage, following tears that were meant to throw whoever I was talking to off balance.

But with people I liked and trusted, I tended to be honest. There was little concern Minato might sell me out, but I never knew who else was listening, even in a place like this.

The finishing touch on my outfit was a black lace mask fitted over the upper half of my face, and Minato wore the same.

Then it was our turn to perform. As the curtains rose, applause greeted us. The sound grew louder when we both were in view, the frame of a mirror between us.

The show started simply enough. Both strolling as if we were walking in front of the mirror, stopping, using each other as a reflection and doing a double take. Mirroring each other's movements.

I loved classic movies, especially the black and white slapstick, and I'd gotten the idea watching Harpo Marx and Lucille Ball.

Unlike in the movies though, the movement was

more sensual and dance-like, and our clothes came off as the routine went on.

The whistles and claps were intoxicating as we showed more and more skin, and the laughs when she would turn away and I would make a face, or we'd interact instead of mimicking, added to the rush in my veins.

I'd forgotten what a turn-on this was. So many eyes on us. Dancing but rarely making contact. Knowing most everyone in the audience was entertained and aroused at the same time. Desire and heat flooded me, growing more potent the longer the show went on. I'd have to take Fen up on his offer after all.

A tiny nagging at the back of my mind said this didn't solve my problem, but sitting on the benches hadn't either, and this would distract me for a couple of hours from the fact that there was a shoot-on-sight order attached to my name.

CHAPTER 2

FREYR

Wonderful thing about being a twin, I shared a bond with my sister that most people couldn't imagine. On the other hand, it also meant I knew when either of us was full of shit—and right now we were both lying to ourselves. Like so many times in the past when we'd had this *discussion*.

"I spoke with Nemain yesterday." Freya—Aya—paced the length of my office, managing to avoid the mahogany coffee table in the middle and the leather couches that lined the walls without ever missing a step. "She's hearing whispers."

Everyone was *hearing whispers*. "And she wants your help."

Her pale hair was the same color as mine, but where I kept mine short these days, hers hung in dreadlocks around her shoulders. Her loose dress hinted at the strong body beneath. The neon accents on the walls reflected off her pale blue eyes and gave her an eerie appearance. "She wants *our* help."

I was unimpressed. Everyone wanted our help. Centuries ago, Aya and several other goddesses of death and war had sealed away their most potent threat—a goddess of chaos who would have destroyed the world if she'd been allowed to roam free.

The act had not only bound Malsumis, but connected her captors to each other. None of them were allowed to act against each other, on penalty of the seal being broken. When one of their own, Hel, was killed, the pact was broken. Now a lot of them were being hunted. Hunting each other.

"I didn't see her answering your call when you asked for it," I said. In fact, when this new threat first emerged, everyone else had tucked tail and hidden.

Not that it did them any good. They'd been captured anyway, and nearly offered as sacrifice. It had been our help—our allies—who rescued the entire group, and Aya nearly lost her life in the process.

She stared at me, searching my face, and I practically heard her thoughts daring me to stay on this path of resistance. "We're past the point where we can say *it's not my problem*. We've been past that point for decades," she said.

She was pushing this because she felt guilty. The pact had kept her from helping her followers, but they came for her anyway when she needed it. They saved her life.

"I'm not saying that." I thought for a moment. "Correction, I am, but only about them. What I'm doing here is protecting people." I was a god of fertility. Of peace. I wasn't made to fight, but I could offer sanctuary to those who needed it. The hunted, the infirm, and the refugees of this war of the gods.

Freya shook her head, her disappointment tangible. "I don't think we're going to have a choice. Soon we're all going to have to fight."

"Spoken like a goddess of war."

She rolled her eyes. "I'll tell Nemain you'll think about it."

"Think about what? What am I supposed to do?" My question landed in the middle of my empty office because Freya had vanished before I finished speaking.

Damn it.

I sank back in the leather and wood office chair that was more than a century old, and tried to find some semblance of mental balance. NEON helped. The desire and appreciation for sensuality that spilled in soothed the cracks in my mind.

None of it erased the core issue, though. Freya was right—we were past the point where the gods could hide in their silos, but that didn't mean I would fight.

A distinct familiar thread ran through the ambient worship from the club. Fresh. Intelligent. Fun.

Dahlia.

Amazing how a not-quite-three-decade-old mortal could bring a smile to my face. Better still, she was doing something that caused more lust to spill from the club and from her.

I tucked my longer term issue aside, left my office behind, and headed toward the back of the main stage.

Dahlia was dancing with Minato, glowing with the *need* that flowed from and to her. Fuck that was alluring.

The show ended, the girls took a bow, and the curtains closed them off from the thunderous applause.

Minato and Dahlia grabbed their clothes and moved out of the way to make room for the next act. When Minato saw me, she gave me a shy *hello*, and scurried past.

I stepped in Dahlia's path, and backed her out of the main flow of backstage traffic. She wore a mask, which did nothing to hide her from me. I trailed a finger lightly under the black lace. "I haven't seen you in here before. Are you new?" Apparently I was in the mood to play.

She caught her bottom lip between her teeth. "It's my first night."

"And I thought I knew all the girls." I skated a hand up her side, barely making contact. She was stripped down to pasties, ruffled panties, and fishnet stockings with garters. The perfect blend of blatant and teasing.

And her shy smile with understanding underneath was the same. "You seem like someone I'd like to get to know."

"I am." I cupped her neck so lightly I felt her heat more than her skin.

Her eyelids fluttered and a soft sigh escaped gently parted lips. "You have to do me a favor, though."

"Anything."

One corner of her mouth twitched up, and amusement sparked across her face. "Don't tell the owner about me. I hear he's a real bear."

I raised an eyebrow. "Wolf, actually."

"Not that owner." She smirked.

I growled. My weak bear impersonation would infuriate most of the berserkers I knew, but her giggle was worth it. I lowered my head to sink my teeth into her bare shoulder. She moaned and her body sagged into mine.

My desire cranked toward maximum, sparking over my skin.

"Oh no, Mr. Deville, not the casting couch again." Her voice was breathy.

This woman, I swore... "Not that it matters, but do you even know what you're saying or are you just stringing words together?"

"Frequently both. I thought you liked that about me." Dahlia straightened.

"I adore that about you. What other kinds of things can I make you say?"

"It's almost always a mystery until it actually happens."

So true. And I was up for the challenge. "Let's take this someplace where we can be loud." I grasped her fingers loosely and led her toward the apartment I kept above the club.

As we walked, the bright aura of seduction that surrounded her faded, leaving enough room for her stress to peek through. That wouldn't do.

I'd met a lot of people in the millennia that I'd been alive. Some were kind. Seductive. Assholes. Killers. But most of them were content to just be. They didn't want to grow beyond what they were on the surface.

But Dahlia was one of those rare souls who pushed so hard to be more, and who wanted to appreciate the world around her. Having her freedom taken from her for so long, when she was with TOM, seemed to amplify her desire to grow.

Sex was wonderful, but taking care of those rare

individuals was important too. I grabbed her a robe when we got inside upstairs. It was too big, and the terrycloth over what little clothing remained from her dance costume made her even more appealing. She was the perfect combination of cuddly and alluring.

She was also fiddling with the ties and casting her gaze at the door every few seconds, as she inched away from it.

"I'm glad you're here. To what do I owe the pleasure?" I said.

"It was convenient."

I squeezed her fingers and she stepped closer. "You just happened to be in Chicago? Try again."

"I'm safe here." She winced as the words passed her lips on hesitation. "Aren't I?"

Her doubt devoured me, but I understood it. She'd trusted before—the people she was raised with, who she called brother and sister—and it hadn't ended well. "You're always safe under my roof." I poured the assurance into my reply. "Talk to me."

Dahlia scrubbed her face. The woman who had been dancing on stage, the trained killer, the confident double agent... those facades were all gone. When she exhaled, the air escaped noisily through her fingers. "There's a price on my head. And I'm meant to know it. I uncovered it in the shadows of the deep web. Magnus is off on some quest with

Kirby, finding more Valkyries, and it still takes me a few days to heal from a paper cut." She worked her jaw, then shook her head and clamped her mouth shut.

And it didn't matter how good she was with a gun or her fists, if she went up against an immortal who could heal instantly, or teleport before an attack connected, she couldn't fight.

I hated to see her like this. "What can I do?"

"Make me invincible?" Her laugh was strained.

"Would that I could." My sister may think I was choosing to sit this fight out, but I was approaching it from a different direction. Someone needed to shelter the less powerful as much as others needed to confront things head on. "You're welcome here as long as you want, though."

Dahlia draped her arms around my neck, and the bathrobe fell open. "If you can't give me immortality, fuck me silly so I forget for a few hours?"

A far better coping mechanism than drugs or drinking, and honestly one of my favorites.

I rested my hands on her hips, nudging the robe open wider, and glided my thumbs up her stomach. In the light, she was a stunning contradiction. The robe made her look small. Timid. But muscle, distinct definition from years of intense physical training, ran through her.

Tiny tassels swung from the barely-there covers on her nipples, and the ruffles on the ass of her briefs were playful. She studied at me with black-lined eyes through heavy lashes, her full lip brightened with violet caught between her teeth.

"You didn't say *yes*." Her voice was deceptively meek. "Do you want me to beg?"

"I might. Not yet, but the night's still young."

CHAPTER 3
FENRIR

After I talked to Dahlia, when she arrived, I tried to force my attention back to the floor. The thoughts that had been nagging me for months surged back stronger than ever. Seeing her hadn't helped, though it wasn't her fault.

I'd spent lifetimes fighting wars, and it grew old. It was part of why I was here with Frey. This place was a safe haven, and the gods steered clear. I'd been happy to settle here. To stop killing except to protect those who couldn't protect themselves.

I was done with war.

Or so I'd told myself.

But the last battle I'd been in, more than a year ago now, with Kirby and Starkad, drew me sharply into my past and reminded me how much I enjoyed a *real* fight.

The entire affair also pointed out that hiding in the shadows wasn't always the best option. No matter how hard I tried to convince myself otherwise, I wanted to join the war again. Be on the front lines. My oath to Frey wouldn't allow that, not without his leave, and I couldn't break that bond, but that didn't stop my longing for a real fight.

The wolf part of me wasn't as tame as I tried to pretend.

When she stepped onto stage with Minato, my thoughts about war and whether or not I missed it faded to the back of my mind.

This place always reeked of desire and sex, but over the years I'd learned to make both a background element.

I could never ignore Dahlia though. And watching her dance, her genuine joy and the heady scent of her arousal that rolled underneath, was an incredible sight.

The dance was familiar—Dahlia and her partner Magnus had brought it to the club a few years ago. I'd never seen anyone else perform it well, though, and I'd never seen Minato do it. There wasn't even another girl scheduled tonight to be her partner.

It seemed odd that she'd decide last minute to make the change to her routine, especially for a complicated dance that required a skilled partner.

The dancing finished and both women left the

stage. As the next routine started, I couldn't shake the odd feeling that something wasn't right.

I headed into the back toward the dressing rooms. As I neared the open door, movement inside caught my attention. Minato had Dahlia's bag in hand, and was opening it. Dahlia was nowhere to be seen.

"What are you doing?" I struck a balance between a casual question and a hint of growl.

She jerked her head up, her eyes wide. "Dahlia asked me to grab her lip gloss for her."

"Why can't she grab it herself?" I asked. This situation was all kinds of wrong.

"She didn't say." Minato strolled toward me, bag in hand. "Will you give this to her when you see her?" She handed me Dahlia's purse and her fingers brushed mine.

Blackness blanketed my mind. I blinked to shake away the nothingness. What was I doing in the dressing room? With Dahlia's bag? I'd been here for... something.

I racked my brain, but no matter how hard I searched, I couldn't grasp how I got here from the front door. It must have been important, but no urgency tickled my senses.

The scent of Dahlia's arousal was back, farther away than before, but not much. If I'd let my desire lead me, that must be why I was back here. I was done working for the night; I wanted to see what she was up to with Frey.

Following my nose brought me to our apartment above the club, and I pushed inside without pause.

Dahlia was sitting in Frey's lap, her robe falling halfway down her back and his hands roaming without hesitation.

There was no jealousy at finding the two of them in the middle of a hot and heavy make out session. I'd fallen in love with a god of sex and fertility and I understood that meant he fucked around. Sometimes I joined him, and sometimes not.

With Dahlia, I was always interested. She was fun and sexy and playful. She'd also said and proved that she didn't have a problem with making a twosome into more, or telling either or both of us *no* if she wasn't in the mood.

I crossed the room in a few long strides, and drew my fingers along her bare shoulder. "Room for one more?"

"Most definitely." Dahlia's reply was breathy. She nipped the back of my hand.

I growled and knotted my fingers in her now-loose hair, tugged her head back, and dipped to capture her mouth and swallow her gasp. I bit at her bottom lip and lingered on her taste. When I let her go, her presence stayed with me, and I moved to crush my mouth to Frey's.

This was the decadence of salted caramel versus the smooth heat of fine whiskey, and the two blended on my tongue and in my nostrils. I was happy to alternate my attention between Frey and Dahlia.

Before I lost myself too much, I forced a reminder through my thoughts—*be careful*. Dahlia was fragile, and it was best to put my mental leash on while I was still thinking clearly.

Frey nudged Dahlia back, and they both stood. He took my hand, never removing his touch from her hip. The living room disappeared and we were in the bedroom, thanks to his ability to phase from one place to another in a blink.

I smirked, letting my hunger show now that we had more room to play, and shoved Dahlia's robe to the ground. Her pasties from the show were gone and her nipples were a tantalizing shade of pink, and still damp and swollen. Frey had been giving them the proper kind of attention.

She was still in the ruffled panties, though. Cute, to be sure, but they needed to go.

I extended enough of a claw to slide the flat surface along her hip, and she shuddered with a delightful moan. With a twist and a tug, I ripped the fabric and tossed the lingerie aside. Dahlia's scent, her desire, was more potent now, mingling with Frey's need and fogging my senses. I wanted to taste her.

I half lifted, half tossed Dahlia onto the bed,

straddled her legs and pinned her arms over her head.

Her laugh ended in a groan as I licked along her neck, and sank my teeth lightly into her shoulder. I should take my time, teasing and kissing over her bare skin, but Frey had already started on foreplay and her musk was too strong for me to ignore.

I kissed my way down her chest and stomach, nicked my teeth over her hip, and spread her legs. *Fuck*, she smelled so good. I held on to enough restraint to keep my fangs from emerging, and licked up her pussy.

She tasted even better. As I devoured her juices, alternating between tongue buried inside her and gliding up to tease her clit, she ground against my face. I was vaguely aware of a naked Frey kneeling next to her on the bed, giving her breasts more attention while she stroked his cock.

Dahlia's pulse was audible and her heavy breathing tantalizing. She gripped my hair with her free hand, holding me in place.

"Oh, *fuck*, please..." Dahlia's cry cut off any other words.

"Please, what, Gorgeous?" Frey's question was low and coaxing.

Her fingers tightened in my hair. "I don't— More. Please?"

I didn't have any restraint left for teasing. I dove

my tongue inside her as Frey pressed his touch to her clit.

The familiar gasps and cries of her coming were a chorus to the way her body clenched around me. I licked harder, savoring her flavor and needing all of it. I pressed in until she shuddered away, and even then it was hard to stop.

Dahlia's body sank away from me, and I forced myself to pull away.

I moved up to smash my mouth against hers, to let her taste herself on my lips, in a sloppy desperate kiss that only paused long enough for her to yank my shirt over my head. My mouth found hers again as she fumbled with my jeans.

I kicked the rest of my clothing to the ground, and my cock sprang up, wanting its own attention. "I need to fuck you." It was hard for me to wrap my tongue around language in this state. I rolled onto my back, pulling her with me. Needing to bury my dick inside her.

Bonus to being a god—no STDs or unwanted pregnancy meant no condoms. I lifted Dahlia enough to position her over my cock, and thrust up. *Fuck* she was tight and slick and a perfect fit.

I glided my hands up her chest, pushing her upright and cupping her breasts. With each tweak or pinch of her nipples she gasped, and squeezed my shaft. Like my own little rubber duckie.

Frey knelt behind her, between my legs. As he

dragged his fingers along her slit, he teased my skin as well. He teased her opening then slid two fingers in next to me, which felt incredible.

I moved my hands to her back and pulled her chest into mine, growling gently at the feeling of hard nipples pressing into my skin.

Frey used his touch to coax and stretch Dahlia open and spread her freely flowing juices around. When the tip of his cock pressed into the base of mine, my anticipation spiked.

He eased his dick inside Dahlia, to rest next to mine. Calling this a snug fit was an understatement, but it felt fucking incredible.

Frey reached between us to tease Dahlia's clit as he and I built to a slow rocking rhythm inside her. The bliss on her face, the way her eyelids fluttered and her chest heaved, pushed me into my own zone of pleasure. Her breath came in short pants, and the world seemed to pause when she climaxed again.

The squeeze of her pussy around both of us was almost too much, but it was incredible at the same time. I came hard, barely aware of digging my fingers into her hips as I spilled inside her. Frey's grunts and thrusts and the fresh slickness said he'd reached orgasm as well.

We lay in a pile in the middle of the bed, sex and sweat heavy in the air, and cut with contentment. We'd have to move soon. Clean up. Wrap ourselves around each other and see if sleep or round two came next.

But for now, this was perfection.

Electricity prickled across my skin, and the atmosphere around us changed. My thoughts flashed back to a cave from more than a year ago, where I'd fought with allies against an insane god and a dragon. My growl and teeth emerged without my permission.

Someone knocked on the front door.

CHAPTER 4

DAHLIA

The dancing and sex had done exactly what I hoped—distracted me for a few hours.

To be fair, calling the sex *a distraction* was an intense disservice to the moment the three of us had stolen from time. My body still hummed with pleasure, I hated that we'd all had to put some form of clothing on, and my legs were unhappy I forced them to work.

As I looked at Frey's visitor, the petite, white-haired woman standing in his doorway, the adrenaline pumping through me now, surging in my limbs and gnawing at my thoughts with a loud *run*, obliterated the last few hours of calm.

Whatever I thought fear and uncertainty were when I arrived at the club, I was wrong. It didn't matter that I'd only met this woman once before, in a bookstore of all places, or that she was shorter and slighter than I was. All that mattered was she was the face from my dreams. The nightmares filled with more death and pain and terror than the whole of TOM had ever delivered.

Fen gave her a short bow, and my world crumbled away.

"Verdandi." His greeting was a combination of deference and disdain.

Neat trick. Not in any way reassuring.

"I prefer Artura." Her smile was soft. Gentle. A lie. Every inch of me knew it.

Frey's face twisted into something that looked like distaste. "Of course you do."

Wait. Verdandi, as in, one of the sisters of fate? Urd's sister. The creature the prophecies were named after. Yeah, the same prophecies that were the reason for me being trained to kill people like Minato.

Skuld's sister. The asshole dragon who tried to kill my friends, because of some fucking series of fantastic stories the three told each other as bedtime stories before humanity even existed.

This woman—beast—was more than the literal stuff of my nightmares. She'd ruined dragons for me. Oh, and as far as I was concerned, shared the responsibility for the gods being at war with each other, and their drive to fulfill her prophecies and see the world destroyed in ice and flame.

"So, I'm going to leave you three to talk. I've got

places to be." Abu Dabi maybe. Was that far enough away? Were those rockets to into space for the typical person yet? I might not be immortal, but I sure as fuck could hack my way into the computer system that would give me a ticket to the moon, if such a thing existed. "I'll catch you both later."

Frey had a back door out of his place, that didn't require me to walk past her to leave, but I couldn't make myself turn my back on those piercing violet eyes. I really should've come here armed. Not that a bullet would hurt a creature like her.

"Actually, Dahlia, I'm here to see you."

The way my name rolled off her tongue turned my gut to lead. How did she know who I was?

Artura looked up at Frey, having to tilt her head back significantly to do so. "I give you my word, I'm not here to harm her.."

He gave a short nod, stepped aside, and gestured for her to enter.

Fucking gods and their fucking assumptions of propriety. I didn't know why she terrified me, but her presence had me wanting to crawl out of my skin to get away.

"I'm Artura. It's a pleasure to meet you." She took a step into the apartment and moved toward me.

If she was who she said, and she seemed to be, Frey and Fen couldn't stop her if she went full dragon. Not that either of them seemed to have any interest in doing so.

"Why are you here?" I asked, since no one else seemed interested in doing so.

Artura studied me. "To meet my niece."

"Excuse me, what?" My question forced its way out because it was easier than letting my brain do the math about what she'd said.

The corners of her mouth tugged up. "You're Skuld's daughter."

Fuck me.

Nope. Hang on. That was bullshit. "Sorry, lady. You've got the wrong girl."

"You've been having dreams."

And now the scary bitch was in my head? "Everyone has dreams. TV taught me if you don't, you go crazy, and I believe everything I see on TV." Did dragons do sarcasm? If not, would she think I was unstable and useless and leave me alone? I was really grasping for a plan here and not finding anything.

"Not those dreams." Artura's reply was soft. Almost sympathetic.

I wasn't buying it.

And then she was right in front of me, with Frey and Fen still behind her. I hadn't even blinked. My terror peaked and I swore my heart stopped. She rested her palm on my cheek.

The images that surged into my mind were like

my dreams, but so much more vivid now that I was conscious. They carried smells—rain and ash and flame and the salt of the ocean. Screams of lust and terror and glee and agony. And so many emotions I choked.

"I can't—" The words clogged my throat, the room spun, and a merciful blackness engulfed my mind.

My world swam back into view from a new angle. One that looked like a ceiling as I pried one eye open. Instinct born of years of training kicked in, and I did as much of a check of my surroundings as I could without giving away that I was on full alert. My head rested against something harder than a pillow but softer than the floor, and was slightly elevated above the rest of my body.

The textures pressing into my skin said I was still in Frey's bathrobe, but a soft plush brushed my hand. Upholstery? And the fingers tracing along my scalp and running through my hair were strong but gentle.

"Welcome back, Duckie." Fen's greeting was a blend of concern and relief.

And apparently they knew I was awake. I opened my eyes and confirmed that yup, my head was on his leg and I was lying on the couch. *What happened?* The cliché question stuck in my throat. I could see Artura a few feet away, and I wasn't giving her the satisfaction. "Thanks."

"I didn't know that would happen, I'm sorry." She sounded contrite.

I wasn't buying it. "Uh-huh." Whatever *that* was. Some horrible ancient-being mind trick.

"I understand Dahlia is something special," Fen said. "But you're going to tell me out of the billions of people in the world, who have come and gone throughout history, that she just happens to be the first one of you to appear since humanity came into existence?"

Plus there was that whole *I'm a wimpy mortal* deal I had going on.

"She's not the first of our children, no." Artura kept her distance, her hands clasped in front of her. Not reassuring given how quickly she'd moved before. "We learned eons ago that we can bear human children. None of them have been like us. There have always only been the three of us, and now that Skuld is gone, the visions say Dahlia will take her place."

The words snagged on my thoughts. "Wait. Back up." I sat, my fear replaced with a creeping anger. "Did you raise any of those kids?"

"No." Artura looked at me as if the question was unnecessary.

The fuck? "So, you're these three ancient beings who think you can see the future of all of humanity—"

"Only some of the more crucial highlights," she cut me off.

I glared. "And you realize one day, thousands of years ago, *oh, hey, we can have babies.* And your next step is to just fuck around at random times and I'm assuming, what, just leave them somewhere?" Did they really just dump all of them, supposedly my *actual* siblings, into whatever system did or didn't exist at the time?

"We've made sure they all had other lives." Artura's reply didn't fill me with confidence.

"Lives like mine? Foster care until some random fucking god decided I might be good enough to kill for their cause? And now you walk in here with some *you're the chosen one* crap?" Now that I was talking, the anger flowed. "*You're a dragon, Dahlia.* Fuck that Harry Potter, Bilbo Baggins bullshit. When TOM took me in, they fed me a similar line. *You can be a hero. You can save the world.*"

"We don't have the power to save the world," Artura said.

Was she fucking serious? I was on my feet before logic caught up with me, stalking forward until I was nose to nose with Artura. "One—I think you're full of shit. I'm not a fucking dragon. I'm an orphan who's sick of self-righteous immortals. And speaking of sick of, I've had it up to here"—I waved my hand over my head—"with prophecies and inaction and doing things just because someone who can blink from place to place said to do them. So you can just fuck off with whatever this is."

Fear and reality caught up to me as the words finished tumbling past my lips. Did I just tell off a dragon? Would she claw my heart out now? Tear NEON apart?

"Please Dahlia, if you would just hear me out." Artura never raised her voice.

So much bullshit. "No. I won't." My insides were jelly and adrenaline and terror, but I wasn't backing down.

"If she's not interested, you need to leave." Fen stood next to me, hand on my shoulder.

"Dahlia." Frey's tone was sharp.

Artura gave me another glance. "It's all right. If she doesn't want to listen, then now's not the time to talk." She turned and walked from the room, closing the apartment door softly behind her.

The moment I heard the latch click, fury drained away, taking my strength with it. I sank to my knees in the middle of the living room. What the fuck was that?

CHAPTER 5

FENRIR

For the second time tonight, I scooped Dahlia up and set her on the couch. At least she was conscious this time, though her blank stare and the faint scowl frozen on her face made me wonder if she was in shock.

I understood where both she and Frey were coming from, the two different attitudes toward Artura. Frey was as much a believer in the ancient ones as his followers were in him. It didn't matter how far the curtain had been pulled back, revealing that Urd and Artura had tossed their words into the world and then stepped back and let the gods tear themselves apart over them. Habits like deference and respect for certain individuals were hard to break.

Like Dahlia, I had a less than stellar opinion of most gods, thanks largely to my lineage. That meant what I needed to say to her was out of concern for her having the truth, and not because I felt she should bow to anyone, including Artura. "Maybe you should've heard her out."

Dahlia blinked away the thousand yard stare and stared at me. "Why?" Her question was flat. "Because she might be family? I'll reach out to her if you're going to call your daddy and tell him you want to reconcile."

I raised an eyebrow. She wasn't too badly shaken if her sarcasm was still intact. Loki was my father, Hel my sister, and I'd spent centuries distancing myself from them and their justifications for who and why they killed. "Because if what she said is true, you may need her insight."

And because I knew what it was like to not have control over one's other form. To lose myself so completely--

"She's got more knowledge than all of us. She came to you in peace and respect," Frey said.

Dahlia flopped into the cushions with a huff. "She dumped me on a doorstep—"

"*Skuld* did that." Frey's voice hardened. "And you already knew Skuld was an asshole."

She fixed her glare on him. "I'm not a dragon. Believe me, I love the idea. Not only is that the ultimate in immortality, but... a fucking dragon. *Wow*." She tugged open her robe to expose her hip, and the darkening marks shaped like fingertips I'd left on her hip. "When was the last time you had a simple bruise stick around for more than a second?"

"I haven't eaten all day. Do you get delivery up here? The kitchen's still open downstairs, isn't I? I'm famished." Dahlia pulled the robe closed again and stood.

The jarring change in subject meant Dahlia didn't want to talk about this anymore. If the situation were any other one of hundreds of thousands of options, I'd let her get away with it. There was no reasonable explanation for Artura's visit beyond the truth, and an inexperienced being wielding magic was one of the most dangerous forces on the planet. I knew from a personal experience that made me ache when I touched the edges of the memory. I couldn't imagine being a dragon lessened that risk.

The conversation wasn't over, but it wouldn't start again if Dahlia shut down. She needed to be guided back to the subject and kept close in the meantime.

"I brought your bag up." I nodded to the messenger bag near the door. "If you want to put on your own clothes, we'll make some food."

"Yeah, okay." She grabbed her purse and headed into the bedroom.

I remembered when Frey gave her that bag. I'd rarely seen someone so excited over something so simple. It was charmed to be able to hold most anything, and she called it her own personal bag of holding. She always carried extra clothes, her laptop, and other necessities.

When she was gone, I let my shoulders slump and turned to Frey. The past called for my attention, carried on my concern for her, and I couldn't find the words to express the gnawing inside.

Frey rested interlocked fingers at the back of my neck, and rested his forehead against mine.

The familiar tenderness was soothing. "We have to change her mind," I murmured as I wrapped my arms around his waist.

He brushed his lips over mine. "We will."

We stood wrapped in each other while I absorbed his calm.

"When you told Dahlia *we'll make you dinner...*" Frey trailed off.

I pulled away with a grin. "I meant you. Yes."

He rolled his eyes and shook his head, his smile intact. "At least start the coffee. We might need it."

"That's fair." I waited for him to turn away, gave his ass a playful swat, and followed him into the kitchen.

We worked in comfortable silence, working with and around each other with practiced ease. Some people were surprised to find out we were in a committed relationship. After being together for hundreds of years, the possessive need to mark my territory by always being affectionate in public had become something deeper and more private.

I didn't care if Frey fucked around. Even if he weren't a god of fertility, I wouldn't have an issue with it, though it didn't hurt that I frequently joined in. I cared that he was mine, from now until the end of eternity.

"Where should we eat?" Frey asked as we finished preparing plates.

"The sun's about to come up in Milan."

He smiled softly. "Done."

I pushed open what looked like a pantry door, to a balcony that sat two stories up, looking out over Italy in the pre-dawn light.

While Frey could create a door to most anywhere on the planet, as long as the place wasn't blocked by a different magic, it worked best if the portal was to a familiar place. We owned property dotted in various places, and this was always one of my favorites at sunrise.

Dahlia joined us, offering a smile though the distant, not-quite-here stare was back. "Thank you," she said softly, and she took a seat. She tugged a smaller chunk of turkey from her sandwich, and pulled off tiny pieces to nibble on.

"It was good seeing you on stage tonight." Frey's tone was conversational.

Dahlia glanced up, then returned her attention to picking at her food. "It was good being on stage."

"Is that why we got to see you? Minato called?"

My concerns from earlier trickled back. The ones I'd pushed aside in lieu of more blatant news.

Dahlia shook her head. "She asked for a favor once I got here, because her dance partner called in, and I can't tell her *no*. But it was a nice distraction."

Her dance partner? Definitely suspicious.

Dahlia picked up half her sandwich, and set it down again with a sigh. "Bragi found us. A few weeks ago when we were apartment hunting. He made it clear we couldn't hide." She poured large quantities of sugar into her coffee, followed by almost as much cream, and fixed her gaze on her spoon as she stirred.

Bragi was one of the gods who ran TOM. A bard and god of music who had become more concerned with his immortality than his believers as time went on. Like most of the gods who sat on the TOM board of directors. It was my understanding Magnus had been close to him at one time, but not anymore.

There was more to Dahlia's story. The same thing she held back when she got to the club.

Frey and I ate, to give her time to fill in the blanks if she wanted. She sipped her coffee. Nibbled her sandwich. Back to the coffee. "I think they're looking for someone outside of TOM to eliminate me. I say *think* because I'm certain I was meant to see the note, so I don't know how much of it was real. It was searchable by my name, and it was poorly encrypted. Enough to keep some skriddie out, but it took me about two seconds to crack. Because the password was *Duckie*." She finished by dragging in a long breath.

A chill ran through me. I called her Duckie because everything seemed to roll off her, like water off a duck's back, and while the nickname wasn't a secret, as far as I knew no one else used it. Which brought me back to my concerns about Minato or someone else inside the club having less than innocent plans around Dahlia.

"I don't know where to hide." Dahlia looked sad. Scared. Frustrated.

"Here. Always. I meant that," Frey said.

And I agreed but, "Maybe hiding isn't the answer."

"Do you want her to wave a flag and say *here I am, come and get me?*" It didn't sound great when Frey put it that way.

But that was my plan. "More or less."

Dahlia's head shot up, she met my gaze, and some of the lines around her eyes vanished. "Because if I keep running, I'll always be wondering where they're going to find me."

Smart girl.

"But if you stand your ground, you know exactly where they'll be looking, and that gives you the advantage."

Frey raised an eyebrow. "What are you going to do?"

"Dance," I said.

He shook his head, and focused on Dahlia. "You looked good on stage tonight, and I'd love to have you up there, but I can also put you someplace no one will find you."

Dahlia turned her attention from me to Frey. "That's reassuring, but also sounds kind of sucky," she said. "I only have so many years ahead of me. I'd like to not spend any more of them cowering because of TOM. But are you talking, we hang a sign on the front door that says *Dahlia's dancing at NEON?*"

I nodded. "Exactly."

Her frown was back. "What if Artura is right and I'm one of them? A new fate? I don't want to be like them. What if I already am and I don't know it?"

Welcome to Tangents-R-Us—population Dahlia. I wasn't complaining. Both conversations needed to be had.

"You can call her back. See if she'll still talk." Frey's tone was kind but firm.

She shook her head so hard I wondered if it might pop off. "Nope, nope, and one-million percent nope." She turned wide eyes on me. "You could teach me, right?"

I wouldn't be able to ignore my own past, my own mistakes, much longer if she kept down this path. But her safety, the world's safety, was more important than my comfort. "How to be a dragon? No."

"How to see if it's true that I am one. Or whatever. I mean, they summon their forms like you do. They can be different sizes, the way you can."

" It may look similar, but there's no way for me to say it's the same. A berserker's change doesn't work the same way mine does. I was born with the knowledge. I knew how to change before I knew how to walk. It's all instinct."

I dragged in a deep breath. "But you do need to learn. If you can't control it, especially if you lose yourself when you shift... It's hard to come back from that." I still had dreams about being trapped inside my wolf. About how close I'd come to surrendering any humanity I had and just devouring anything in my path, even if it meant the world burned.

CHAPTER 6

FREYR

Racks of costumes stretched out in front of us, offering a vast assortment of lace, satin, and leather. Some of the dancers made their own outfits, but I had plenty on hand as well. I wandered up one row and down the next, Dahlia by my side and Fen standing watch.

"Do you have a preference?" I asked.

"Black?"

I glanced at her *Hackers Do It with Their Fingers* T-shirt, and the way it bled into a matching black skirt over even blacker leggings. If I could blend that look with the burlesque theme, it'd be fascinating to see her dance in it.

"How about, tell me if anything grabs your attention," I said.

It had been late when we pointed Dahlia toward the guest room and told her to get some sleep last night. Letting her stay here—keeping her here—was for her safety and everyone else's. If she shifted, it might wreck the house, but I'd be close enough to take her someplace remote to deal with it.

I hoped. Skuld had the ability to keep people from phasing in and out of places, but I was operating on the assumption and hope that was a learned skill and not something she'd invoke at random.

"This is pretty." She was holding up an all black dress trimmed with violet

I didn't like the idea of her doing this—dancing as a way to draw out her foes, telling Artura off, or ignoring her potential heritage—but I understood the whys behind all three. And if this was the path we were on, if we were putting her name on our club, she was going to be the best headliner we'd ever had.

The dress Dahlia had was attractive, but it wasn't unique. "All of it or just bits? Pick out what you like, we're having you something custom made." If I stared long enough, something would inspire me. Something unique to her.

After she'd retired to her room last night, Fen and I headed to bed too. A lot of immortals could forgo sleep for days if needed, and we could as well. But I was a big fan of shedding everything and wrapping ourselves in each other and blankets, and replenishing our bodies and souls.

This news was gnawing at him. The pain of the past was reflected in his eyes.

It was still there this morning, as he watched us, watched the world around us, and was on high alert for anything.

"I can't believe I'm getting my own personal cosplay tailor." Dahlia dove back into the racks, enthusiasm radiating from her.

The outfit would determine the dance, though I was already running through those possibilities as well. After long enough I lost track of time, we had a short stack of dresses, with her favorite piece from each, draped over chairs near Fen.

"Strip." His voice was growly. He did that so well.

Dahlia smirked. "Yes, that's part of the show."

I raised an eyebrow. "So you can try on the outfit."

"Yes, sir." Her sass was tangible.

I smacked her ass, as motivation, the sound echoing through the room. She tried unsuccessfully to hide her soft gasp of pleasure behind a giggle.

The way she undressed was an observation in seduction. There was no hesitation, and her movement was fluid and graceful. She knew she was being watched, but she wasn't overtly performing.

As she bent at the waist to push her leggings to the ground, white flashed to view behind her.

That was it. The perfect dress and show. I gathered up everything we'd just picked out and set it aside. "Stand by."

She only wore a bra and panties, but she stood in the middle of the floor, hands on her hips and impatience etched on her face.

I stepped past her to grab the dress we usually used for bachelor parties. It was meant to be a *wedding* dress, but I had different plans for it.

When I turned to face them again, Dahlia's eyes grew wide and her hand flew to her chest. "Now? Me? I never— That is..." The breathiness in her voice was exaggerated. "I mean, of course the answer is *yes*. I don't want a big wedding, though. Only one or two hundred of your closest friends. Gift cards on the registry—I do *not* trust gods to shop for video games."

Fen almost cracked a smile.

I chuckled at the antics. "You're sorely misinformed if you think 200 gods are still speaking to me on terms that involve inviting them to a wedding."

"I don't know," Fen said. "We could pretty much count on a Maleficent situation in that case. Macha storms in, curses someone. Those assholes decide it's a sign and ban gods from touching spinning wheels for the next two centuries. TOM and FU have a new reason to fight. Could be good for a laugh."

"The dress isn't for a wedding." I was both amused and concerned about the potential accuracy of the scenario Fen laid out.

Dahlia's bottom lip quivered. "What? But I though…"

I dragged my thumb along her pout, and the fake drama faded into a sigh as she parted her lips. She didn't resist when I pushed into her mouth, and she sucked playfully before letting me go.

She was too much fun.

"Wait for it." I moved to a box of accessories and extracted a collar with a chain, and a gold bikini.

"No." This time Dahlia's surprise sounded real. She got it.

"You need to shine if you're going to headline. The dress is just to get an idea, I'll have one made without all the ruffles. We'll do an entire Star Wars theme," I said.

She clapped. "You're seriously the best."

Fen cleared his throat.

She hugged him. "Both of you."

Dahlia stripped down to nothing and put on the gold bikini. She had the skirt on as well, when a loud, "Hello?" carried back from the front of the club.

"Magnus." Dahlia grinned and half-sprinted, half-skipped to the main room of the bar.

Fen growled. "She's impossible sometimes."

"She's fun, and this was your idea."

He sighed heavily, but he wasn't as bothered as he pretended. We followed the same path she'd taken, to find her embracing another woman. Magnus had been Dahlia's partner when they were with TOM, and they were closer than any sisters, despite the bumps in their past.

"Did I interrupt something?" Magnus nudged Dahlia back to arm's length and swept her gaze up and down.

"I'm going to be Princess Leia." Dahlia sounded pleased.

Magnus patted her on the head. "I'll come back when the three of you are done role playing. Or... whatever this is." She turned away.

Dahlia grabbed her wrist. "Knock it off. Stay. We have to catch up about *a lot.*"

"We only have a few hours for you to start practicing before the club opens." Fen's stern tone wouldn't sway them if they weren't in the mood, but I appreciated that he tried.

Magnus paused and turned to us again. "Practicing what?"

"I'm going to be Princess Leia."

Magnus pursed her lips at Dahlia's response. "So you said."

This was silly, but also not getting us anywhere. I pulled out a chair near the stage, and gestured. "Have a seat, Magnus. You'll see."

Fen took the spot next to her.

"You, come with me." I jerked my thumb toward the stage.

Dahlia bit her bottom lip. "Here? Now? With such a small audience? Our timing's not that good."

It took a second for her response to click. "Not that kind of coming. Not unless you behave."

I cued up the music from Jabba's throne room. We'd have to modify both feature name and song enough to avoid copyright issues—even the gods didn't dare face Disney lawyers—but this would do for now. For the next couple of hours, Dahlia and I worked through the basics of a dance, while Magnus and Fen watched and offered suggestions. Some helpful, some not so much.

I was glad Magnus was here, and hoped we could get her to stay. Having a Valkyrie on guard, especially one with modern military training and who Dahlia trusted, gave us one more person to keep an eye on things.

I hated the nagging voice that asked if any precautions we took would be enough.

CHAPTER 7
DAHLIA

I could pretend all I wanted that everything was fine, that putting on a pseudo Princess Leia costume was a dream come true, and that my being here was a happy fun vacation, but if I stopped and thought, even for a moment or two, reality crashed back around me.

The instant Frey gave his permission to help ourselves to the liquor, Magnus was behind the bar. Where I'd fallen in love with the dancing when we tried to infiltrate this place, she'd been drawn to the bartending.

She flipped the bottles in the air, caught them behind her back, and mixed drinks with flair. And she glanced at me every few seconds the entire time. She wasn't buying my *everything's awesome* act any more than I was.

Magnus set our daiquiris on the table, and took

the seat next to me, across from Fen and Frey. "I was worried when I heard the rumors about Dahlia."

"What rumors?" Frey asked.

"Same thing I found." I wasn't surprised. Magnus had a similar and complimentary skillset to mine. It was part of the reason we'd been paired as a team. We were shitty killers, but we could do brutal things with and to a person's digital footprint. "It's why we decided I should dance," I said to Magnus.

She frowned, but a smile quickly replaced the look. "Bring them to you. I like it."

"You'll be sticking around for a while, I hope," Fen said.

Because of course he did.

Frey nodded his head up. "We have a spare apartment you can stay in."

Magnus furrowed her brow again and looked at me. "I was thinking of going home. I assume that means you're not joining me?"

The men thought I hadn't figured this out. "Fen and Frey think I'm a dragon and that I'm going to lose control in the middle of the night and hurt someone. So they're keeping a close eye on me."

"That's not—"

"That's about right." Fen cut Frey off.

Magnus's jaw dropped. "A *dragon*? Holy shit. You didn't lead with that? Hours ago? How the fuck are you a dragon?"

"I'm not." I might be. The idea terrified me. "Do

you remember the dragons? The one you helped stop? My daddy-slash-mommy?"

"Ah." Her face fell. "That kind."

"Is there another kind?" I didn't know of one. Then again, a year ago I didn't know dragons existed at all.

Fen shook his head. "I hope not."

"I was kind of hoping there was." Magnus shrugged. "But you don't have to be an asshole like them, just because you're related. Fine, the dragon thing isn't awesome. It's wrong that being a dragon isn't awesome. When do you make your big debut?" She gestured at the stage.

Voices besides ours flitted through the room as people trickled in for work.

"The sooner the better," Fen said.

I agreed. Best to get this out of the way. It was mildly terrifying, but in a way I was familiar with, and this was something I could control. I was desperate for any illusion of control.

Frey tapped his forehead. "I'll have The Tailor in here tomorrow for measurements, and we'll kick off the rumor mill announcing our new secret star. Costume should be done in a day or two, that gives Dahlia and I time to polish the routine and practice, and she can open three nights from now."

"Awesome." I meant it on some level, even if I couldn't push the enthusiasm into my voice.

Frey pushed back from the table. "We have work

to do. You ladies are both welcome upstairs, down-stairs, wherever you're most comfortable."

I heard the creak of a door, and a movement out of the corner of my eye caught my attention. The world seemed to slow to a crawl as a figure appeared out of nowhere, behind Frey.

The new arrival was holding a pizza box. Did we order in? I recognized him. What was his name? Something slipped past my lips, but I couldn't hear it.

He dropped the box at the same time he drew a gun from a holster under his jacket. My training kicked in before my reason. I screamed, *"Get down,"* as I ducked and turned the table on its side between us and the attacker.

Not that this table would stop a bullet.

Why wasn't anything happening?

Why was everyone staring at me?

"What are you doing?" Magnus asked.

Heat flooded my face. There was nothing wrong, was there?

Frey studied me with concern, and I swore I could feel Fen's tension radiating from him.

"There was— Didn't you see—?" Pain pulsed behind my eyes while adrenaline and fear raced through my veins over a threat that obviously didn't exist. "I swear I saw someone..." Oh, fuck. What was wrong with me?

"Take her upstairs." Fen's tone was sharp.

Magnus shot him a withering look that my thoughts were too muddled to make sense of. I didn't have the strength or presence of mind to argue as she helped me up to the guys' apartment.

I sank into the couch and dropped my head into my hands. The cushions next to me shifted with Magnus's weight and she leaned into me with a light nudge.

"What happened down there?" Concern lined her question.

"I saw something. Someone... It was so real."

"I believe you. I promise you there was nothing there, but I believe you saw something."

I sighed and raked shaky fingers through my hair. I trusted Frey and Fen, but there were times they looked at me and saw an inexperienced and naive little girl. Given I was thousands of years younger than them, I didn't blame them, but it meant there were some things I was more comfortable discussing with Magnus. She *got* me.

"I didn't come here because of the contract on me," I confessed. The news sucked, but it was confirmation of something Magnus and I were already pretty sure of. "I've been having dreams. Vivid. Intense. Terrifying. And last night, this woman showed up here—Artura. She's one of the dragons and she's the one who told me I was too, and then she touched me..." My head throbbed harder at the memory and I winced at the pain.

"Headache?" Magnus asked.

I nodded.

"Let me." Valkyries had the ability to heal. I'd been so jealous when she became one and I couldn't, but over time I'd grown okay with the whole thing.

She brushed her fingers over my forehead, and sharp sparks seared my skin. The pain intensified instead of vanishing as I jerked away. "Ow. What the fuck?"

Magnus frowned. "I don't... I can't. It's not working."

"Be right back." I stumbled into my room, dug a bottle of ibuprofen from my purse, and swallowed four dry. Why couldn't she heal me? What was going on?

A nagging voice in the back of my head had the answer, but I didn't like what it was saying so I ignored it.

"Downstairs." Magnus's voice came from behind me. "What happened?"

I turned to find her standing in my doorway. "It was like my dreams, but I was awake. It was so vivid." Because Artura was right. "I think it might be true." There was no relief in saying the words aloud. "I think I might be a dragon. Or at least, have some of their powers. But I don't want to be bound to visions for the rest of my life. I don't want to bind other people's futures to the things I see."

"Like what?" Magnus prodded. "What was in the dreams?"

"What makes you think it was anything worth mentioning?"

She gave me a look that was half *duh* and half *because I know you, bitch.*

I sank to the edge of the bed. "I keep having one, over and over, and it's so vivid I can hear it and feel it and it clogs my nostrils and chokes me when I wake up. So many people die. Fen dies. But I can't ever see why. It feels so real, though..."

"And that's why you came here," Magnus said.

I nodded. "I had to make sure he was okay, as ridiculous as the notion was. And then Artura showed up, and the vision I saw when she touched me..." A shudder ran through me as the images solidified in my mind. "It's me. I'm the one who kills—killed—him."

"And that's how you know the visions aren't always true." Magnus sat next to me again. "Because you would never. Not him."

She was right, I wouldn't. So why was the fear so very potent?

CHAPTER 8
DAHLIA

Emotions clashed in my mind. I should be terrified. Running on adrenaline and unable to climb down from the high.

But I was in Fen and Frey's apartment. It was safe here. *I* was safe here.

Fen sliced my skin deeply enough for me to draw in a sharp hiss that blended with his growl. He dipped his head and licked along the rapidly vanishing cut.

That shouldn't turn me on, but fuck if it wasn't hot in this moment. "Again." My request came out as a sharp whimper, and I peeled back enough of my top to expose the top of my breast.

Frey's breathing was jagged.

There were no claws this time. Fen went straight to a sharp bite that made me gasp in surprise, and followed with his rough tongue, bathing the instantly healed skin.

He moved his mouth to mine, kissing me hard as he gripped my hips and lifted.

I wrapped my arms around his neck and my legs around his waist, sinking into the primal desperation that flooded me.

Fen's growl hummed through me. "If you're not fragile, I don't have to be gentle."

I liked the sound of that. Each desperate bite broke my skin, leaving behind a sting that lingered longer if I focused on the tantalizing sensation. He slammed me against the nearest hard surface—Frey's chest—and captured my mouth in a ravenous kiss that crushed my lips against my teeth.

As mouths clashed and hands roamed, I'd never been touched more thoroughly—groped more completely—while completely clothed. I swore if I twisted my body right, rested against the right hard topography on Fen's body, that I could grind until I came.

"Where would you like to go tonight?" Frey's question rumbled through my skin.

I knew without asking what he meant. "Las Vegas. Top floor... anywhere."

His chuckle was fuel on the raging fire inside. "Pressed against the glass, backlit, for a city full of nightlife to see?"

"Yes, please."

With his hands on my hips, he lowered me to my feet. The three of us made quick work of stripping down to nothing, then Frey took my hand and led me to a window that had appeared at the far end of the living room.

Neat trick. One of my favorites.

He kept me facing the glass and pressed into my back, his erection leaving an impression on my behind. Lights twinkled from the city below, and we were high enough up it was unlikely anyone could see details.

But they'd see a silhouette and know what was happening. The thought sent desire crashing over me and pulsing between my thighs. Frey honed his touch in on the source of my need, stroking and teasing lightly over my slick skin and swollen clit.

Fen stepped up next to me, and pressed a hand to my throat, squeezing enough to tempt and fuzz my thoughts. He forced my gaze to his. "The things I want to do to you... The ways I'm going to ravage you... There's not time for them all tonight, but we can get started."

"Promises, promises." I tried to keep my tone playful despite the roaring heat consuming my senses.

Fen tightened his grip ever so slightly. "Damn right." He nipped my bottom lip hard enough to break the skin, then licked it clean. Over and over, until my mouth tingled and my head swam, and then he crushed his mouth to mine.

Frey traced circles around my clit, pressing in tighter the faster my hips bucked.

Fen forced my feet apart, making my balance precarious. He shoved his free hand between my legs, and thrust three fingers inside me, stretching me out with the sudden penetration.

The angles shouldn't work.

I didn't care. I was floating away in a wash of pleasure and pain and hunger and salvation. Climax surged inside, shoving away everything else, and orgasm crashed around me. I didn't care about the rest of the world. The only thing that mattered was right now.

A tremor of pain thrummed under my skin, jarring me from the bliss, and I grunted in surprise. Another shock jarred my senses, tearing a small whimper from me. This wasn't the kind of pain Fen was inflicting this bordered on agony. My body shuddered away from them, but the pain didn't subside.

"Duckie?" Fen's concern hung in the air.

I could *taste* it. How was that possible?

The next spike of agony jarred me into a rigid and upright position. It felt like razors slicing along my skin. Like someone was taking a ball peen hammer to my shoulder blades and coccyx.

I held my arms in front of me as black patches of

scales appeared on the backs of my hands, my forearms...

This was not a kind of pain I liked.

A new level of torment racked my tailbone, as if I'd been knifed in the lower back.

Spots swam in front of my eyes, shifting into images. Shapes that were as real as anything in the room. As I looked down, a vision of my limbs becoming scaled dragon arms and legs overlapped my real body. I was large enough to fill the room and still be on the bed simultaneously. Wait, I hadn't been in the bedroom.

Fen sat on the bed in human form, comforting me with Frey. But he also stood in front of me, a giant wolf, teeth bared and ears back against his head. He backed up as I moved closer, his growl low and threatening.

Shadows I couldn't identify loomed behind him. A threat. If I didn't stop this, I'd die instead.

"I don't want this." My protest came out as a screaming roar. I swiped a claw and sliced his flank before he could lunge aside.

No. I didn't want this. It wasn't real. I could see *real* on the bed. But I wasn't a part of it.

My scream jarred me awake, and I jerked upright in bed. When my eyes flew open, the dream still lingered in my vision. My heart hammered against my ribs and my pulse roared in my ears.

I held my hands up. The patches of scales were

still there. My ass hurt. A tail flicked against my legs, and I felt the contact on both sides.

The images of me launching at Fen clouded my vision, overlapping with him in my doorway, teeth bared and face somewhere between wolf and human.

I didn't know which version of him was real. Were any of them?

CHAPTER 9

FENRIR

Frey was by my side as we burst into Dahlia's room. I had no idea what we'd find, but her scream yanked out every *fight* reflex in me. I was ready to tear the throat out of whomever hurt her that badly.

We pulled up short when we found her alone on her bed, knees hugged to her chest and tears spilling down her cheeks.

She looked up, but her gaze stared past us, to something I wouldn't see if I turned. Patches of her skin shifted from flesh colored to violet to black and then back again, and a scaly tail wrapped around one of her legs.

I felt Frey's tension. He was ready to move us away from here at a word. I rested my hand on his arm and shook my head slightly. Magic could make this worse, or startle her. Blinking to a new location was a last resort if I couldn't talk her down.

I stepped forward and she scooted back on the mattress.

"No, no, no, no, no," she muttered. "I'm sorry. Please don't."

Whatever happened, she was still lost in it. I approached as slowly as I could, with her moving away until her back hit the way, her *I'm sorry*s spilling out over and over.

"Dahlia." I touched her arm softly.

She jumped, but when she looked at me, some of the focus returned to her gaze.

"Are you real?" she asked.

Had she been dreaming? Having visions? The patches on her skin and the tail said she was stuck mid-shift, so it made sense she'd be having other side-effects.

"Yes. I'm real. So's Frey."

"Did we have sex? Just now? Like dirty, hard, cutting sex?"

That must've been some dream. Though, I wasn't impressed if it left her in this state. "No. We didn't have any kind of sex tonight."

"Do you remember earlier today?" Frey's voice was low and even. "The Princess Leia outfit? Magnus is here?"

She nodded, and some of the tension seemed to drain from her body.

"This is real," I said. "We're real. You're real. Whatever you saw before we got here, it wasn't."

Dahlia loosened her arms and crossed her legs. "I don't know if a dream would say that." Her tone was lighter. Not joking, but no longer terrified.

"Did your dreams tell you they were real?" I risked sitting next to her, and let out a soft sigh of relief when she didn't move away.

She shook her head. "I didn't think to ask, though."

I wanted this to be all soft warm fuzzies, but I couldn't help with what came next unless I knew what had happened. What triggered the fear and partial shift? I could try to keep the conversation light, though. "Dirty, hard sex, huh?"

"You were happy I wasn't fragile anymore."

I would be, but I didn't want her to linger on that thought. "I'm happy you're all right."

"Am I though?" The patches of scales had settled on her skin, and the tail had stopped flicking.

Frey stepped up to my side. "You are. You're all right. You're safe. Does it hurt?"

Dahlia followed his gaze, her eyes growing wide. She held her arms up in front of her, turning them back and forth. "That much is real. I guess it wasn't *all* a dream."

The threat was lessening with each passing moment, but it wasn't gone. Especially if she was unaware of her physical state. "Duckie? Does it hurt?"

"I don't... No. I guess not."

Unsettling thing to be uncertain of, especially given her blood curdling screams. How hard did I want to prod for details?

"I'll put some coffee on." Frey squeezed my shoulder.

I grasped his hand long enough to kiss the back of his knuckles, then let him leave. He closed the door on his way out, which meant he was planning on being able to change where the exit led if he needed.

"It's real, isn't it?" Dahlia looked at me. "Not here, in this room. I believe you when you say it. But..." She held up her arms and flicked her tail. "I'm a dragon?"

She should be saying that with joy, rather than terror.

"Unless you've pissed off someone who cursed you, it looks like it's real." I tried to tease, but my joke felt flat.

The corners of her mouth tugged up anyway. "Honestly, I'd be surprised if I haven't pissed someone off that badly by now."

I trailed my fingers lightly along her arm, over the distinctly different textures of flesh and scales.

She jerked away with a shudder.

"Does it hurt?" I had a feeling I'd be asking that a lot during this process.

"No. But I feel it all, no matter where you touch. Like it's all a part of me."

"It looks like it is."

"How do I make it go away?"

I smiled sadly. "I don't think you do." She needed to come to terms with this change sooner rather than later. Preferably now.

"I mean how do I control it? How do I choose for my skin to be skin again at this moment?" She raised her hand to her scalp then paused and examined the back of her hand, before raking her fingers through her hair. "You said you were born knowing how to change, but you have to have noticed something over the years. You have control over when your teeth come out. Your claws. How big your wolf is..."

How was I supposed to answer her? "Do you think about breathing?"

"No. But when I want to hold my breath I think about it. You can't tell me that *big wolf, small wolf, scary fangs only* aren't at least a little conscious."

I supposed that was true. "In that case, I'd do exactly as you said."

"I'm trying. I'm thinking *go away you stupid fucking scales. I don't want you here.*"

Not quite the level of acceptance she needed. "I don't fight my wolf. I accept that it's a part of me."

Even as I spoke, the words tasted like a lie. But they'd always been the truth.

She huffed and flopped onto the mattress on her back. "I can't accept this."

I tugged her into a sitting position again. When I ran my thumb along the black patch of scales on her hand, she tried to pull away.

I gripped tighter. "Do you remember when you learned dragons are real?"

"Yes."

"How amazing you thought it was?" One of the things I adored about Dahlia was her enthusiasm for things I took for granted. Her smile lit up the room when she discovered dragons were a thing.

Now she was frowning. "Then I learned who they really are. What they are and aren't responsible for."

"Ignore that for a minute."

"Hey, brain, stop thinking about the fact that three omniscient beings wrote down the future of humanity and the two who survived do nothing to stop the zealots from killing in their names." Sarcasm dripped from her voice.

Her statement was a series of half-accuracies and misstatements, but now wasn't the time to nitpick details.

"Go back to the fantasy of what you expected from a dragon," I said. "Don't you want that?"

She shrugged. "But it's not reality. *Fantasy* being the key word."

"Make it reality. There are only two other dragons, and they don't get to dictate who you are. No one can convince me that you haven't been the one to shape the direction of your life. It doesn't matter how many people tried to steer you toward their goals, you're here now because of *you*. Defy the world again." The statement came out more passionately than I intended, but I meant it. Dahlia was her own person.

She sighed, but her smile was back. "How?"

"I'm making this up as I go along, but my guess is, if you want to be that dragon, close your eyes and picture yourself becoming that dragon." It was a starting point.

Dahlia closed her eyes and seemed to turn inward. The seconds ticked away. Nothing was happening. The creases in her forehead said she was aware. Her breathing was labored.

The black spots grew so slowly at first I thought I was imagining it. As the scales spread across her skin, awe raced through me. I was glad she wasn't looking, because I didn't know how she would react, but the sight was stunning. Onyx glinted with violet in the dim light, her fingers lengthened into claws, and wings tore at the back of her shirt.

The door clicked as Frey returned with two mugs of coffee.

A whimper tore from Dahlia's throat, and every hint of dragon receded into nothing.

Frey frowned and set the mugs on the end table next to me, apology for the interruption clear in his eyes. "This changes our plans for you headlining."

"No it doesn't," Dahlia said. "TOM is coming for me, and they don't care what condition I'm in when they get here as long as I'm dead before they leave."

"I'm not putting you on stage if you can't control this." Frey managed kind and concerned mixed with firm.

"I'll get it under control." Dahlia's voice was hard.

If this deteriorated into an argument, there was no telling how difficult it would be to get Dahlia back on track. "Keep making arrangements," I said to Frey. "Dahlia and I will keep working on things on this end." All the security needed to be in place regardless. I agreed with Frey that she couldn't perform in this state, but it hadn't been thirty minutes. We had time to figure things out.

Frey nodded. "I'll put most of the pieces in place, but I won't make the headlining announcement until we're certain."

Dahlia scowled. "I'll be ready."

I grabbed Frey for a quick kiss, and he left us again.

"He's right." Dahlia's soft voice drew my attention, but it was the hint of resignation that drilled through me. "I can't... I don't have control."

"You will." I had to believe that, and I needed her to believe it, or it wouldn't be true.

She shook her head and dropped her face into her hands with a half-sigh, half-sob.

"You woke up screaming," I said. "Was it pain?"

"No."

I placed a finger under her chin and raised her gaze to mine. "Tell me."

"Earlier tonight—yesterday?—when I freaked out in the bar? I had, I don't know what to call it, a waking dream, I guess. Of a guy pulling a gun on us."

That explained the behavior. "Okay." I didn't want to say anything to stop her talking."

"I've had other dreams. The one that woke me up, it's why I came here. It's why..." She dragged in another shuddering breath. "I saw myself transform. Become a dragon. And..." She pulled away from my touch. "And I killed you."

I hadn't seen that coming, but I hid my shock. "That's not you."

"You don't know that."

"I do." And I was going to do everything in my power to keep things that way. For my sake and hers.

CHAPTER 10

FREYR

Magnus stood at the top of a ladder, fiddling with an *Exit* sign with an arrow pointing toward the nearest door. The trick was, the vents in the bottom held a camera behind them. "How about now?"

Dahlia held a tablet with an image on the screen that was the room we stood in, but from Magnus's perspective instead of ours. She pinched and zoomed and rotated the image. "I think that's it."

"Perfect." Magnus hopped from almost a meter up and landed deftly on her feet. "Next?"

Dahlia jerked her thumb toward the main room. "Behind the bar should give us a good angle."

I'd never had security cameras before. I'd never needed them because I knew who was coming and going and no one found the place unless I wanted them to.

That used to be the case. My sister had been kidnapped out from under my nose in this bar, and many nights there was a malicious presence, but I couldn't pinpoint who the feeling came from.

"Can you do weapons?" Magnus asked as the four of us including Fen headed to the liquor shelf behind the bar. She flicked her wrist and a dagger shimmered to life in her hand. She twirled the blade a few times with the deftness of someone who'd been raised to be comfortable with knives, then tossed it up in the air, where it vanished in a sparkle of magical glitter.

Dahlia shook her head. "How would I hold a weapon?"

Early this morning, Fen gave me the remaining details of how things went with Dahlia, from her struggle with transformation to the dreams. Dahlia told Magnus the same story, but with a lot more *I had wings* and a lot less *I woke up screaming and terrified because I dreamed of ripping someone apart with my teeth.*

Now the women were comparing notes about what their nifty new powers could do. Magnus had been a Valkyrie for a year, so she'd had more time to get used to the form. She'd also adapted almost immediately and had someone training her who was familiar with how things worked.

"I'm just saying, if a dragon doesn't have opposable thumbs, are they really all that evolved?" Magnus stepped up to the bar.

"No." I pulled her back.

"That's the best place for the camera," Dahlia said.

Which was fine. It wasn't that I didn't trust Magnus with the liquor bottles—I'd had far less skilled people working the bar—but this was still my domain, and I still controlled the way things worked here. "And I'll let you put the camera there." I waved my hand over the wall, imprinting the order of the bottles, and whispered a mental command to send the liquor to a nearly identical shelf setup in a currently unoccupied suite in Las Vegas.

"Neat trick," Magnus said.

Fen set the ladder down next to where she stood. "I'd like to point out that a lack of opposable thumb doesn't make one less sophisticated."

Magnus climbed up a few steps, grabbed her bag of tiny cameras and tools from Dahlia, and set it on the top of the ladder. "I mean, on an evolutionary scale, technically it does."

"A human evolutionary scale doesn't take gods into account." Fen's tone was casual but the snarl he finished with was intimidating, as was the snap of his elongated teeth and snout. Experience told me he was joking. Mostly.

"I had thumbs last night." Dahlia flexed her fingers in front of her face, and a flicker of black rolled over the back of her hand, her fingers elongating and gnarling for a heartbeat before returning to normal. "But the claws and such aren't really made for holding... anything."

Did she do that intentionally? That was still my biggest concern—she may be calmer but that didn't indicate she had control. What Fen told me about Dahlia's dream terrified me. I'd seen the final result of a prophecy be different than interpreted, typically because language changed over time, but there wasn't a lot of variation in *I killed you.*

There had to be more to the visions than that. Surely some never came true. Dahlia was still human. Perhaps Artura had given her bad dreams.

I very much wanted to believe that, but I couldn't.

"I shouldn't look the gift of potential immortality in the mouth. Though if dragon teeth are involved..." Dahlia shook her head. "I think I'd still rather be a Valkyrie though. You have a much cooler queen."

Magnus wrinkled her nose. "She hates being called that."

Dahlia grinned. "I know."

And that was as malicious as I'd ever seen her—joking about calling someone royalty who disliked the mantle. She'd been trained to kill—had killed—but I also felt what kind of heart she had. I couldn't sense all emotion, but her terror last night over the vision, dream, whatever it was, had been tangible.

Magnus positioned the tiny camera on a shelf. The device's size made it impossible to determine where she was pointing it. "How are we looking?"

Dahlia swiped and poked the screen of her tablet. "You have the doorway up to table six."

"One more or two?" Magnus asked.

"One will give us a decent overlap." Dahlia pointed at the display behind Magnus. "Let's put it two shelves higher."

Rather than hopping down, Magnus summoned her wings and hovered a few feet off the ground while Fen moved the ladder to where she indicated.

"Show off," Dahlia grumbled.

Which made me wonder, "Why do you need the ladder?"

"I can't do this all the time." Magnus made the answer sound obvious. "It would be tacky and excessive."

Dahlia huffed. "Whatever. In keeping with the Star Wars theme, blowing up the Death Star."

The statement wasn't as out of context as it sounded. She and Magnus played a game that was essentially *how would the story have gone differently if the gods wrote it.*

"First Death Star or second?" I enjoyed the randomness of this, combined with pop culture references that spanned decades neither woman had lived through.

Dahlia twisted her mouth and didn't answer for a moment. "Second."

"To start, the Ewoks would've been vicious little man eaters." Magnus positioned the next camera.

"Not necessarily. It depends on which god is responsible for them," I said. "They may be a tribe of body positive, sex loving nudists. They obviously understand clothing and choose not to wear pants."

Fen raised an eyebrow. "I don't believe the god matters in this case, and I do believe they could be both."

Magnus seemed to consider this. "I agree. How do we look?"

"Y'all are a bunch of perverts and sociopaths." Dahlia studied her screen. "Three degrees left and a notch up. And that's not the Death Star."

"Says the woman helping install cameras to keep people out," I said. "The tech is part of the equation. And if the Ewoks are the monsters you say, would the storm troopers really have survived long enough to install the shields on the moon?"

"Would the god in question have cared?" Dahlia didn't look up from her screen. "Set on that camera."

"Hold up," Fen said. "Is the god writing the story or playing the emperor?"

Magnus grabbed her bag and hopped down, landing softly on her feet. "If a god is writing the story, of course they're playing the emperor. Self-insertion of the most obvious kind."

"Are the Ewoks involved in that as well?" I had to know.

"Sure." Dahlia grinned. "One big orgy of man-eating furries and mutual masturbation."

I shook my head, but I was smiling. Potential concerns about her losing control aside, I did like having her around. "I think we lost the plot"

"That implies we had one to start with." Dahlia closed the cover on her tablet and stashed it in her bag. "You can bring the top shelf booze back now."

I reached for the bottles mentally, the way someone would if they knew exactly where in their pantry the sugar was kept. Nothing was there.

It wasn't that the bottles were missing from where I expected them to be, rather where I expected them to be was missing. I couldn't sense anything outside the bar. Discomfort climbed through me. This was, I expected, like a person who could see their entire life waking up blind.

"Unless you wanted to dust first." Fen's tone was flat.

The sensation was disconcerting, but the fact that I'd experienced this before, when a pissed off, burned out dragon had us trapped in a series of caves, cranked my internal alarms to blaring. I looked at Dahlia, who was sifting through her bag.

She looked up, and her eyes grew wide. "Was he right? Do you want me to dust? Earn my keep?"

"No." I frowned.

Could she be doing this?

"Do we need more cameras?" Magnus asked. "You wanted to wrap up before people started arriving, and that's soon."

No god of sex would ever admit he couldn't get it up. I reached out mentally again.

The liquor was exactly where I expected it, with no magical void pinning me to one spot. I phased the bottles back onto their shelves. Was the whole thing a fluke?

Fen studied me with curiosity and concern.

I made a faint gesture, to indicate we'd talk about it later. If Dahlia did that, it must have been subconscious, and if she was projecting that kind of power now, she was more dangerous than I feared.

"We having a party?" Minato's voice came from behind, catching me off-guard. How did I miss a single person approaching the club? Especially one with a mild magical aura.

Magnus vaulted the bar more smoothly than any Olympic gymnast. "Nah. We were going to raid the expensive booze, but we got caught."

Minato wrinkled her nose. "Why? They would've given you some if you'd asked."

"Where's the fun in that?" Magnus countered.

Minato looked disgusted. Was she buying this?

"Glad you're both here now." She sounded very much like she didn't mean it.

After Dahlia and Magnus hunted her, then decided not to, they still told her who she was and why she had a target on her back. They figured it was best she be warned, and I agreed.

Since, the three had been the kind of friendly that allowed a performance like the one Minato did with Dahlia the other day to spark with fun and chemistry.

"Anyway. Work calls." Any disdain vanished from Minato's voice, and she headed toward the back.

Or I'd imagined the tension the same way I imagined being unable to find the alcohol.

But both were very real, and I couldn't shake the feeling Dahlia was the common link.

I had agreed to bring parts of this war between gods to our front door, but I wanted Fen as far removed from it as possible. Was that an option anymore? There was no telling what would or wouldn't trigger the events in Dahlia's dream, and with no knowledge of how a dragon's visions worked, I could only do what my instinct told me to. Second-guessing wouldn't serve anyone. "Would you excuse me for a moment? I need to make a call."

CHAPTER 11
DAHLIA

One minute we were having fun, joking about Ewok sex, and then Frey was acting weird. Minato was acting weird. Uncomfortable sparks were dancing over my skin and reminding me that my skin and hand had shifted to dragon without my permission when my jealousy peeked through over Magnus's powers.

I didn't like this.

"Anyone know what that was?" I asked. "Any of it?"

Deep creases marred Fen's forehead. "Something's not right."

"Hence the question." Magnus joined me.

Fen's frown deepened. "I'll talk to Frey when he's done. Keep an eye on her."

On Minato? Forty-eight hours ago I would've asked *why*, but a little extra paranoia and questioning my reality seemed like a good idea about now. Never expected to want *more* paranoia than TOM had imbued me with, but here we were.

"Let's take this someplace less public." Fen jerked his head toward doors leading to back rooms.

The disquiet inside meant I wasn't even in the mood to ask if he was propositioning us. "Yeah. Good call."

Fen, Magnus, and I headed toward a small lounge tucked away from the bar. This corridor used to lead to an entire little town, but Frey had cut off the doorway between the two places to keep the people who lived there safe.

The room was filled with couches and beanbags, and meant for comfort and relaxation. I picked my favorite couch, but the calm I hoped for was far, far away.

I didn't mind that Fen settled next to me, his arm and thigh resting against mine. He might be this close to keep an eye on me—there was no way the men had dropped their concern over my freak out last night—but I didn't mind that either. His nearness and strength were comforting. Soothing.

"Cameras won't be enough. I can't watch the entrances and..." He sighed heavily.

And keep an eye on me at the same time. But I could get this under control, with a little practice and patience. I'd learned to use my body and mind as a weapon when I was barely a teenager. I could figure out how to stop myself from shifting into a different shape.

"Put me on stage. Then I'm in the main room when you are." I understood Frey's concerns, and if I thought about them too much, the fear would over-whelm me. But TOM already knew I was here. They must.

Every reason Fen had the other day for my performing was still valid. My dancing put me in charge of my own destiny and it would make TOM pause. Sure, we—they—were trained to deal with targets in public, but they had to be more careful about it these days. Their connections in law enforcement and other places had dwindled as their structure fell apart. And more gods were actively looking to interfere with TOM activities.

"We'll go ahead with the performance plan, on one condition." Frey's comment from the doorway startled me.

I'd be bothered that he snuck up on me, but he was standing in front of us. I was more off my game than I wanted to admit. "What condition? What changed your mind?"

"You're right. This is the best way to do things."

I typically liked hearing *you're right*, but this felt wrong. Frey had been reluctant from the start, and whatever happened in the bar couldn't have changed that. I was supposed to believe he'd walked away for a few minutes and magically decided this was all a good idea? He'd spent lifetimes avoiding the war between gods, and now, *it'll be fine?*

"What's the one condition?" I asked again.

Frey clenched his jaw.

If I weren't in a room of friends, I'd be wishing I had a gun on me. This wasn't right.

The shadows behind Frey shifted and tension cranked through me. I felt the twitch at my shoulder blades and the itch in my fingers to grow.

Artura stepped into sight. "I'm here."

"You're earlier than I expected," Frey said.

That fucker. How dare he? "I told you *no*." I couldn't keep the betrayal from my voice.

"I made a different decision." Frey didn't meet my accusing glare. "Hear her out. That's my condition."

"So much bullshit." There was Magnus, echoing my thoughts as usual.

Artura whipped her head in Magnus's direction, and her neutral expression shifted to a snarl. A threatening growl echoed through the room, aching in my ears.

"*Defiler.*" Artura lunged at Magnus. "How *dare* you?"

CHAPTER 12

FENRIR

I was shifting and lunging between Artura and Magnus before my mind caught up.

Magnus was already in full armor. Though I knew from the fight we'd had with Skuld that a dragon could do a lot of damage to a Valkyrie.

"*Enough.*" Dahlia's voice was half roar, half panic, and overlapped the way Frey's command boomed through the room.

"You are a guest, as are they, and this is our home." Power rolled off Frey in waves. "How dare you?"

Terrifying. Which was fucking sexy.

Artura pulled up short of attacking one of us, and whirled to face him. She still wore a human form, but her skin was all scales—white and pearlescent—and her fingers were long, gnarled claws. Her tail coiled, ready to strike.

"How dare *you*? You bring me here under pretenses of peace while she flaunted my defiled gifts? While she wears befouled portions of me? I am more powerful than all of you. Older than the two of you combined." Artura's presence seemed to fill the room, though she remained the same size. "I will not—"

"Excuse me." Dahlia interrupted Artura. Would this be her once she learned control? "If you're talking about the ring, I never meant offense. I picked it as a gift for her, and she's more family than you'll ever be. If you don't like the enchant, remove it. It's just a ring."

How did Dahlia do that? Go from a mortal just trying to survive to fearless when Artura was around?

Artura focused on Dahlia, the dim lighting causing dark rainbows to race over her armored skin. "It's not *just* a ring, and that's not *just* an enchantment."

The voice screaming *fight, protect, kill* in my head hadn't quieted. Were we talking or removing a disrespectful guest from the premises?

The energy that rolled from Frey magnified my instincts. He hadn't touched this type of power in centuries. "She obviously meant no offense."

"Ignorance is no excuse."

"Is it a reason to foul a home you were invited into?" Frey demanded.

This wouldn't get us anywhere. I could attack, or I could say the one thing that may work, but would piss off Dahlia I didn't even like the way the words tasted. "Your visions showed you working with Dahlia, or you wouldn't have come here for her." It took focus for me to say so much at once, and I may have reverted to the old tongue at a few points in the sentence.

Artura stepped up to me with a quiet roar. She was more than a head shorter, and my wolf was convinced I could snap her in half with my jaws. "You know nothing of my intentions, boy." Her voice was in my head as much as aloud. "However, I will speak with Dahlia and I'd rather it be with her permission."

"Then don't attack my friends," Dahlia said. Patches of onyx decorated her skin, looking more like spots than armor made of scales. "At least tell us why you're pissed off."

"This is the most valuable thing I own." Magnus worked her fingers in a wave, showing off the full finger ring she wore around ring finger. "It doesn't matter what it's worth—nothing means more to me."

"Of course not." Artura stepped away from us, but didn't return to a full human form. "The fae magic wouldn't work under any other circumstance."

I wasn't ready to back down. "Explain yourself." I let the growl enhance my demand.

Artura focused a glare on me. "The ring is made of one of my claws, which makes it receptive to certain magical energies. I *sold* it to Dahlia for a pittance because gifting it carries consequences, but I recognized she was one of ours and I liked her. Before you ask, I didn't know who she would become. As for the enchant, it's blood magic."

"A meaningless human term." Frey scoffed.

"A very real term when the entirety of a fae is used to imbue a magically receptive item. But the magic should have faded." Artura spoke with disdain.

Horror splashed across Magnus's face, and she removed the ring.

I understood. "Unless the item was gifted with genuine love"

"I've been wearing dead fae?" Magnus's voice was suddenly tiny; a sharp contrast to the battle maiden she presented as.

"Whoever imbued that ring for you knows more, and is more dangerous than you realize," Artura said.

Vidar. Magnus had told us he was the one who made it possible for the ring to hide her from detection and teleport her from place to place. He was one of the gods who sat on the TOM board of directors. More than a year ago, he'd taken a large number of fae captive, and not all of them had been rescued.

Death was one thing, but slaughter to steal magic, to enslave a portion of their being in inanimate objects? The notion made me ill.

"I didn't know. I'm sorry." Dahlia's unstable transformation flickered in a dizzying display.

"Now you do." Artura finally let any trace of dragon fade away, and was human again.

I was still ready to strike.

"You and I will speak." Artura took Dahlia's hand. "And then you and I will be done with each other."

They vanished as I lunged. A blur raced past me, and I chased as Magnus stopped immediately in front of Frey, magical spear to his throat.

"You let her take Dahlia." Magnus pressed the weapon in.

I understood the sentiment, but I also knew why Frey did what he did, and she wouldn't hurt my mate. I grabbed her wrist and squeezed. "We'll get her back."

"I promise," Frey added. "You may not believe this but I made the call for Dahlia's sake. I won't let anything happen to her."

"You just did," Magnus said.

"No. Dahlia is safe." I had no doubt. The knowledge didn't stop the animal inside from snarling and snapping for a way to pursue her and get her back.

CHAPTER 13
DAHLIA

The back lounge of NEON vanished and I found myself standing in the middle of a bookstore, a human-again Artura next to me.

I'd only been here once, but I vividly remembered her bookstore in Spain. Who would forget a place called *The Dragon's Hoarde* that was filled with the glorious scent of old paper and magic? She'd better not ruin bookstores for me the way she had dragons.

And if I focused on my irritation and fascination, I could block out my mounting terror enough to hide it from the scary woman who tried to attack my best friend, then kidnapped me. Swallowing my fear to make a point—Hel would be so proud of me.

"I acted poorly back there; I apologize." Artura's contrite tone caught me off-guard. She gestured toward the end of the aisle we were in, and a doorway I hadn't seen before. "Would you like some coffee?"

Where did the scary human-dragon hybrid go?

I wasn't stupid, but I was having a hard time keeping up. Caffeine would either kickstart my brain or my paranoia, might as well find out which. "Sure."

I followed her into a room just big enough for two overstuffed chairs, and a table between them. She waved her hand, and a tea set—coffee set?—appeared in the middle of the table.

"Can you summon coffee out of midair?" I apparently had no idea how amazing dragons were.

Artura gave me a funny look, and chuckled lightly. "No. I had this waiting upstairs, on the assumption I'd be hosting you as a guest."

She poured dark liquid into each cup. "Cream and sugar. Do have a seat." She gestured at two separate dishes and then the chair across from her.

I sweetened and lightened my coffee significantly—I may be a trained killer, but I wasn't a psychopath—and perched on the edge of the chair. Why did the calm bother me so much? Oh, right, because this deceptively tiny woman looked ready to rip out Magnus's throat less than ten minutes ago.

Artura sipped her coffee. Her black coffee. "You can relax."

"I really can't."

She held out her hand to show Magnus's ring

resting on her palm. "I truly am sorry about my reaction. For centuries, certain gods have sought parts of us—claws, shed skin, hair, scales, you name it—to imbue in vile ways. It's caused us a lot of pain, as well as whichever other beings they use in their enchants. I saw your friend, and I made assumptions."

"Oh." That sounded too reasonable. "I promise I didn't know, and if Magnus says she didn't, that's true as well."

A small ball of flame appeared in Artura's hand, and when it burned out the ring was gone. "Yes, we can summon fire."

"Do we breathe it?" Damn it, I didn't want to get sucked into my fascination or admitting I had anything in common with her. I was also still furious at Frey.

"No. But it looks like we do to the unfortunate who see us summon it." Artura settled deeper in her chair, sitting with her legs tucked and crossed under her. The cushions almost swallowed her up. "You're not supposed to do that." She nodded at me.

I held one arm out in front of me, and frowned at the scaly patches rolling over my skin. "I'd rather not be. Did you do something to me when you touched me?" Besides give a horrifying level of depth and realism to what had previously been a vague dream.

She let out a long sigh. "I meant to give you more clarity with your visions. That was it. Enough to help you see they were real. When Freyr called me, I realized my mistake."

"I'm sorry what?" I leaned closer, pointing my ear in her direction. "Did you just admit to being flawed?"

"Of course I am. No being is perfect."

Was it wrong that her offense made me smile a teensy bit? "So you brought me here to teach me how to use my powers?"

"This isn't one of those ridiculous movies, child. There's no montage for becoming powerful. You simply are or you aren't."

I flexed my fingers and willed claws into sight. Or, I tried. My middle finger extended and then the shift faded and my entire arm was human. "Obviously that's not the case. This must be difficult for you to understand, seeing how you've been *you* since birth, which was an eternity ago. I was born human. I've been human for the last twenty-six or so years. I wasn't anything else until Skuld died, you said so yourself. So how do I do this dragon thing?"

Artura shook her head. "I'm sorry. That's the only answer I have. *You just do.* Do you remember learning to walk?"

"Then that's it. I'm on my own." I puffed out my cheeks and exhaled noisily as they deflated. At least Fen had tried.

"I'm sorry."

And now we were back to the bullshit. "As sorry

as you are that gods are killing each other, and innocent mortals, because you and your sisters told each other a bunch of fairytales before humanity existed? As sorry as you are that your daydreams have become self-fulfilling prophecies and an excuse for wholesale slaughter? That ring you took from Magnus existed because you predicted a bunch of gods would die, and they're willing to enslave and destroy anyone if it means keeping that from happening."

"Urd and I learned a long time ago that things only get worse if we interfere. It's best to let people do what they will, and stay out of their way."

"Too bad you didn't figure that out before you wrote down all your little fantasies and the world got their hands on your words."

"You don't like what Skuld did."

I glared at her. "You're right, I don't. They manipulated two sides into ensuring the *prophecies* came true, because they bought their own press release."

"The prophecies happen regardless. We can warn people, we can keep them to ourselves, it doesn't matter. When we don't get involved, fewer people get hurt."

"I suspect it's more that when you don't get involved, you don't have to admit how many people get hurt." I knew this whole *come on in and have some coffee* was too good to be true. "I refuse to believe that because three beings have vivid dreams, key events in the future are fixed in stone."

"It doesn't matter if you believe it." The edge returned to Artura's voice. "You'll see in time that it happens regardless."

No. I wouldn't. Because my fate wasn't any more set in stone than anyone else's. "Send me back. I'm not your problem."

"Obviously you are."

I shook my head. "I absolve you of whatever obligation you feel. You ignored me for the first part of my life, go back to doing the same now. *Send me back.*" The command came out with more force than I intended, carried on a rumble that shook the floor.

Frey appeared at my side, and anger mixed with shock painted Artura's face.

What the actual fuck?

"Are you all right?" Frey's focus was on me.

I was more than relieved to see a friendly face, despite my irritation with him for putting me in this situation. "No thanks to you."

"You're not welcome here." Artura's sweetness was gone, and the monster she'd become at NEON was emerging.

Frey settled a hand on my shoulder. "Then we'll be leaving."

Artura appeared immediately in front of me, the way she had in their apartment, and grasped my wrist. Her fingers dug into the tendons, sending an ache through my arm. "Then we're done."

My vision swam toward black then to blinding white and back again. I wanted to say *not a problem*, but the words stuck in my throat.

The room vanished and Frey and I were back at NEON.

My vision solidified, but the rest of my body shook so hard I thought I might rattle apart. I sank to the floor, the gloriously solid and familiar floor, wrapped my arms around my knees as I hugged them to my chest, and squeezed tight to keep from falling apart.

It didn't matter that three pairs of eyes probably stared at me; collecting myself was all that mattered. My fear would overwhelm me if I gave it focus. My body and mind felt wrong, as if they belonged to someone else. This was being drunk and tripping on acid simultaneously, with my nightmares—my entire subconscious—vying for domination and my carefully crafted self-restraint slipping into numbness.

What did Artura do to me? What was it about her touch?

Nobles don't lose control. Hel's voice crackled in my skull. I breathed deeply, and again and again, stopping myself short of hyperventilation.

Familiarity flowed through my veins and I focused on it. On *me*.

As the rest of the world swam in, I became aware of everyone else. Magnus crouched next to me, hand on my arm and concern on her face. Fen kneeling in front of me, my fingers grasped between his.

"Dahlia." Frey's concern was tangible.

Fuck him. I shot him the most venomous glare I could muster.

"Are you here now?" Magnus asked.

I nodded, surprised when my head reacted the way I wanted.

Fen studied me. "What happened?"

"She touched me." As far as I could tell, that triggered the nightmares last time, and the feeling of my own body trying to run from my mind this time. I tugged gently away from Magnus to extend my arm and hold my hand in front of my face.

The sensation of there being more to me was gone. I pictured myself with scales. Claws. A tail.

Nothing happened. While I hadn't had control before, I could feel those parts of me.

"What's wrong?" Fen tugged the fingers of my other hand, drawing my attention.

"She took it away." It was the answer that made the most sense, though the words made me sadder than I expected. We always want what we can't have. I turned my gaze to Frey again. "Congratulations, you win." I didn't try to hide my bitterness.

CHAPTER 14

FREYR

When Artura and Dahlia had vanished, it wasn't just from the club. Dahlia was completely gone from my radar, as if she'd ceased to exist.

It was a similar sensation to what we saw fighting Skuld. To what I experienced with the liquor in the bar just a short while ago. There was nothingness in the world when I extended my senses to find her, and an unfamiliar panic gripped me.

What had I done?

Then, abruptly, I sensed her again, as if a wall of brick crumbled.

Watching her now, uncertain, scared, and furious, I ached on her behalf. "This isn't what I wanted." My words sounded weak to my own ears.

She looked past me, to Fen. "I'm going to stay

with Magnus tonight." The emotion was gone from her voice and her gaze was vacant.

"Of course." Fen's tone was sympathetic.

Dahlia shook her head, accepted Magnus's offer of help up, and the two of them left the room.

Seeing her like this, defeated and withdrawn, and knowing that I was at least partly the cause, gnawed at me more than I expected. Even given that she was a good friend. An impulse surged inside to do whatever it took to make this right.

Unfortunately, I was missing a solution.

"I'm not hitting the floor tonight. You?" Fen asked.

I shook my head. A drawback to immortality were those rare moments when I felt my age. We moved up to the apartment as I struggled to collect my thoughts.

"I understand why you called Artura." Fen settled on the couch and I took the spot next to him. "But you had to know..."

That Dahlia would be upset. "I did. I assumed the ends would justify the means. I don't like this outcome, but I don't regret that I made the call."

"I know. If she doesn't vanish in the middle of the night, she's going to insist on dancing. You gave her your word."

It was still a bad idea, but if she no longer had access to her power my bigger concern about her lack of control no longer mattered. "I'll let her."

"Do you think Artura really cut her off from her dragon?" Fen almost sounded horrified at the thought.

For someone so accustomed to his other form, I saw why. "It seems like it. However, whatever's going on with Dahlia, if Artura won't help her, you may be her only chance to make sense of any other form she may have."

Fen dragged his fingers through his hair with a shuddering sigh. "I'm going into this blind, but I'll do it for her."

"We'll figure it out." I had little faith in anything, but when it came to Fen, I never doubted him.

Somewhere along the way, Dahlia had earned my trust as well. She still made some decisions I disagreed with, but she was young and missing some experiences.

I stood and pulled Fen to his feet. "Come to bed."

He chuckled. "It's only eight, old man."

"It's three in the morning in Madrid."

Fen shook his head with a smile, and took the lead as we headed into the bedroom. We shed our clothes and climbed into bed.

He moved around behind me for a moment before spooning me and pressing into my back. The nearness was soothing, but I wasn't a god of nearness. Sex was restorative, and it was more potent than most people would believe when combined with the love and adoration that connected me to Fen.

He glided slick fingers along my skin. I wasn't surprised that he'd grabbed lube before joining me. He teased my opening with a liberal application of lubricant while his cock hardened against one ass cheek.

Anyone else, at any time in history, and I did the fucking. Not with Fen. Not with my wolf. He nudged my hole and I relaxed to let him slide inside me.

We lay there for a moment not moving, and I relished the vibrations flowing between us—both the physical connection and the spiritual.

Fen's first thrusts were slow, a long pull out before gliding back in. As he built to a faster pace, his body slamming against mine, my desire surged and energy flooded me.

He bit my shoulder, hard enough to break the skin, and the shock made my cock jerk with need. The way he dug his fingers into my hips and slammed into me harder and faster, told me he was lost in the pleasure.

I restrained myself as long as I could, finally caving to need and fisting my shaft. I stroked myself, squeezing, working my hips in time with Fen's thrusting. Fucking my hand while he fucked me.

I forced myself to pause when his familiar grunts grew deeper and wilder. He shuddered as he spilled inside me, and his release unleashed my own. I stroked my cock, pumping until I couldn't hold out anymore, and crying out when I came.

When my body shirked from my touch, I had to stop. Our heavy breathing was the only sound in the room as we lay wrapped in each other, him softening inside me, and bliss blanketing us both.

It was always easy with Fen. Always right. After so many centuries, we understood each other without words. That had always been a bountiful gift for me.

So why did my worries about Dahlia linger in my thoughts even now?

CHAPTER 15
FENRIR

I knocked on the door to Magnus's temporary apartment with one hand, and balanced two coffee cups in a holder, with a bag of fresh pastries in the other.

Being raised by TOM meant a steady diet of protein, fiber, and carefully monitored carbohydrates. The diet of a body honed to be a weapon, rather than that of a teenager with an overactive metabolism who wanted to try everything.

Dahlia never passed up sugary and sweet these days, and I hoped the breakfast would make her more receptive to finding a common ground with Frey.

Magnus opened the door, stepped aside, and grabbed one of the coffees as I walked past. "She says to tell you she's still not speaking to him."

"I figured as much." I re-balanced the tray to adjust for the change in weight.

"Oh, Vi... God. This coffee is *amazing*." Magnus's groan from behind me bordered on orgasmic. "Did you—"

"Stop in Venice before I came over? Yes." I moved the pastries out of her grasp before she could grab them from behind. "Dahlia gets first choice."

Magnus huffed and strolled past me to perch on the arm of the couch. "Which god do I have to argue with to get chocolate croissants hand delivered to me?"

"A different one than you've already pissed off. There are enough for both of you."

"Get your ass out here," Magnus yelled.

I could be irritated with the behavior, but it was refreshing to be in the company of people who were comfortable with each other.

Dahlia wandered into the living room, damp hair hanging in dark curtains around her face, and her heavy eyeliner not completely hiding the circles under her eyes. "Morning." She gave me a tired smile.

"Morning." I handed her the pastry bag.

She shook her head and pushed it away. "Not hungry."

Magnus sigh-growled.

I extracted the largest croissant from the bag and

held it close enough for her to get a whiff. The sweet was still warm. "Just a taste."

"Fine." She leaned in and took a bite, chewed, and swallowed. "Maybe I'm a little hungry." She took the pastry from me.

Magnus grabbed the bag from me, and I handed Dahlia her coffee.

"Thank you." Dahlia managed a tiny smile between devouring the food and washing it down.

Good first step. I opened my mouth.

"I'm still not talking to him." She spoke before I could.

I'd suspected this would take time. I could exercise a little patience. "Just think about it."

"I thought about it. Nope." Dahlia took a long swallow of coffee.

"He's going to let you dance," I said.

She raised her brows. "You mean he was actually honest about something?"

My patience cracked at the thinly veiled insult. "I won't do this with you. You can be mad at Frey, that's your right, but don't speak ill of him. I won't let him do so to you, either."

"Did he try?" Uncertainty slipped into her question.

"No. He wants to make things right." I softened my tone again. "You're going to have to work with him to refine your dance."

"Pretty sure she can choreograph a simple stage show on her own," Magnus said.

I had no doubt, but that wasn't the deal. "It's still our club, and we still have the final word on what happens on our stage."

Magnus's phone rang and she wandered off as she answered.

I was focused on Dahlia. "You have to agree to that."

"That wasn't part of the original deal."

"I've altered the deal. Pray I don't alter it further." I winked, knowing she would recognize the quote and hoping she'd see the teasing.

She shook her head, but one corner of her mouth tugged up. "Fine. But that doesn't mean I have to talk."

Getting her in the same room as Frey was a starting point. It was hard to define why this was so important to me, but I couldn't let Dahlia and Frey stay at odds.

"That was Kirby." Magnus walked back into the room. "She says she's got a lead, but I'll tell her *no* if you need me here. Say the word."

Dahlia twisted her mouth and it was a moment before she responded. "I'll be okay."

Magnus frowned. "I can't get there. My ring's gone."

"Frey will drop you off," I said.

"Maybe playing taxi will help him feel some humility," Dahlia added.

Unlikely. "He's downstairs waiting for The Tailor. We can pull him away for a few minutes."

The women finished their breakfast, and we walked down a floor. Frey was in a room set away from the club that was large enough to dance in without having to worry about obstacles. He looked up when we entered, and Dahlia scowled.

"Can you give me a lift to Topeka?" Magnus asked.

Frey frowned. "Kansas? I suppose if you really must."

"I really must." Magnus turned to Dahlia, eyes wide, and jerked her head in Frey's direction.

Dahlia pursed her lips and shook her head.

Magnus did the nod thing a few more times.

Interesting. I was calling them on this. "We can both see you, ladies. It doesn't matter if you're not saying anything."

Dahlia's nostrils flared and she glared at Magnus. "I don't care if you're buddy-buddy with every other immortal you meet. Older does not mean wiser."

"But it frequently does," Magnus said.

Something told me this was a replay of a conversation they'd had multiple times, and rehashing it wasn't changing anyone's mind, but I did want to hear the details.

"Does wiser mean more deceptive? Meaner? More callous?" Dahlia asked.

"Not always," Frey said.

She didn't as much as glance in his direction. Her attention stayed on Magnus. "Vidar gave you a ring imbued with the soul of a tortured fae. Hel... If I start on her list of flaws, we'll be here for weeks. My own family dropped me on someone else's doorstep because they were too *wise* to care that their fucking makes babies. And you're hanging around with the new and improved Rescue Rangers, so now you think everyone older than two-hundred is okay? Starkad tortured us in school."

"Starkad taught us hand to hand combat." Magnus didn't flinch. "He was harsh, but he was always fair."

Dahlia's scowl deepened. "Yeah. They're all great. Go. Have fun."

Magnus studied Dahlia, then gave her a quick hug. "Be careful."

"I will." Dahlia's tone softened. "You too."

Apparently that was that. Frey took Magnus's hand and they vanished.

Time for a little bluntness. But only a little. I turned to Dahlia. "I'd like you to try stashing the *woe is me* for a minute or two, if you can."

"Excuse me?" Shock rippled from her.

"I get it. The gods are assholes. Frey and I both get it, and it's why we do what we do."

"If this is a *just get over it* speech, I'm not interested."

"It's not," I said. "I will never disagree that your upbringing was horrific. I'm surprised more of you don't need intensive therapy." They actually probably did, but a lifetime of *never show the world how you really feel* had far reaching effects.

"I've gone to war with the gods for the man I love, and I'd do the same for you." As the words passed my lips, I tasted their potency. They carried more weight than I'd expected. "But I can't protect you from yourself if you choose self-destruction. Frey didn't do any of those things you were talking to Magnus about."

"You're right, he didn't." Dahlia's concession surprised me. "But he did make that call to Artura after I asked him not to.

He made a judgement call, to protect you.

I didn't get the words out because she wasn't done talking. "And he *was* deceptive about it. He snuck away. He didn't even tell you, did he?"

I was grateful the answer was *no* because the last thing I wanted to do was lie to Dahlia, or have been complicit in a lie. But I'd never questioned him not telling me—he made a decision he knew I'd see the reason in. "Immortals do have experience. That doesn't mean we're flawless. Obviously."

She huffed out a tiny sigh in response.

Frey appeared in the same spot he'd left

moments earlier. "The Tailor will be here soon. After you're done with him, we'll refine your routine."

"All right. Thank you."

I managed to hide my pleased shock that Dahlia replied. I understood both sides of this disagreement, and things would be so much easier if they did as well so we could move past it.

The Tailor arrived. I wasn't sure what kind of supernatural creature he was, besides *fabulous*. Today he wore red and blue hotpants, a satin spaghetti strap tank top, and had streaks in his hair that matched the shorts.

Dahlia remained tight-lipped through most of the measuring. The silent treatment was frustrating, but the lack of sound made it easy for my mind to wander to other portions of the conversation with Frey last night. If Dahlia did have access to the dragon part of her still, which I suspected was the case, could I teach her to embrace it?

I didn't know.

Dahlia was acceptably polite and charming with The Tailor, though I watched Frey's frustration grow every time she brushed his words aside.

The Tailor finished his work and his tools vanished. "May I speak with you for a moment, my dear?" He extended a hand to Dahlia.

"Of course." She let him grasp her fingers and lead her away a few meters.

As they spoke in words hushed enough even my

sensitive hearing couldn't pick up the conversation, my curiosity grew. It wasn't a long talk, though.

They rejoined us. "I'll be done in two days." The Tailor handed Frey a stiff fabric card that would serve as a receipt of sorts, then vanished.

"What was that about?" I asked Dahlia.

She worked her jaw, glanced at Frey, and said, "Nothing."

I wouldn't play games with her if she was withholding important information, but I'd let her simmer on her decision a little longer before I pushed the issue.

CHAPTER 16

DAHLIA

When The Tailor pulled me aside, he asked, "What are you?"

"I don't understand." There were a lot of ways I could answer his question, but the way awe lined his curiosity made me think none of them were right.

"All of my gifts are centered around appearance," he looked me over as he spoke. "And I can see the same in others. I know Fenrir is a wolf from looking at him. But you..."

My breath caught. Could he see the dragon? Was it there after all? "Yes?"

"Your aura is a stunning prism of possibility. As if you could look like whomever you want."

"I do?"

He nodded. "I assume, from what I see. You didn't know?"

I shook my head.

"If you're going to perform, it will be a neat stage trick. But I do hope you'll explore it thoroughly."

Me too. "Thank you."

I wanted to tell Fen when he asked, but I was still upset with Frey and not ready to let his deception go. However, I did obey when he said it was time to practice. It was almost second nature, no matter how hard I'd tried to escape—a god said *do* and I said *on it*.

"Do you want to go over what we practiced the other day?" Frey asked.

He was being kind, and I'd have to communicate with him to get anywhere. "Yes."

Fen started the music, and I summoned the existing choreography to the front of my mind. Or I tried to. It wasn't a complex dance, but I couldn't get the rhythm right with the cantina band. I skipped forward a step too soon, then swung round a quarter twirl too much.

"Are you all right?" Concern peppered Frey's question.

I didn't sleep well last night. The excuse came easily, but didn't feel right. I also wasn't giving him the satisfaction. "I'm fine. Just warming up."

"All right."

I could feel Fen's gaze boring into me, but I didn't dare look. I took the routine from the top.

And stumbled over my own feet on my first twirl.

Then again. And again.

With each stumble or missed step, a new self-recrimination bounced in my thoughts.

I could've been a dragon. I could've been one of the most notorious hunters. I could've been omniscient. A killer. A daughter...

But I couldn't be any of those things because they weren't me. Even if I wanted them, which I didn't, I was a child surrounded by gods.

The thing I hated the most about all of that was the bitterness in my own thoughts. That and the lack of control I had over my destiny.

"Dahlia." Frey's bark cut through my wandering thoughts.

I couldn't hide my wince, but I did manage to swallow my *I'm sorry*. I wasn't wilting under this pressure.

He sighed softly. "This isn't working. How would you like to do things differently?"

My mind froze on the question. What was the right answer?

This wasn't school. This wasn't the past. He didn't want a *right* answer, he wanted my opinion.

But did he? After last night, could I be sure that mattered?

I hated feeling like this. That I couldn't move past these doubts. That he'd lied to me. I pushed resolve to the front and adopted a straight, rigid posture. "I've got it. Let's take it from the top."

"All right," Frey said.

Fen restarted the music, and I flowed into things. The steps were easy. I didn't have to take off my clothes during practice, I just had to sway with the music. I could do this in my sleep.

My toe caught on the floor and I stumbled.

"Damn it, you fucking know this." Frey's sharp tone sliced me to the core.

I was a grown-ass woman and I wouldn't cave to the child whimpering inside me. But I also couldn't summon a response.

"Stop. Music off." Frey scrubbed his face. "I won't apologize for the call I made last night."

"Fine." Wonderful. Fantastic. Fuck him.

"But I am sorry about the results, and I'm very sorry I was dishonest about my intentions." Frey sounded sincere.

I didn't like everything he said, but I did believe him. The hurt wasn't gone, but it was soothed. "Okay."

"Come here," Frey said.

I stared back.

"Now." His tone was firm and commanding, which spoke to those insecurities clawing at me from the past, but it was also kind. A reminder of why I'd come here in the first place. Frey wouldn't hurt me. I *knew* that.

I stepped closer.

Frey grasped my fingers, spun me as he pulled

me to him, and pressed into my back. I stiffened at the abrupt contact, until his warmth spread over me. This was intimate. Safe.

He rested his hands on my hips, and some of the tension drained from my neck. The room changed. We were in a large dance studio with a hardwood floor. There was something freeing about not being surrounded by NEON.

Frey settled his mouth near my ear and murmured, "Forget the routine for a moment." As he talked, he moved my hips, and I felt him swaying behind me to the same motion. "Just focus on feeling your body." He glided his palms up my sides, our movement never stopping, lifted my arms and moved his hands out to meet mine.

A smooth guitar chord filled the room and bled into the faster *Whenever, Wherever* by Shakira.

The external stimulus, the calmness and security of it, made it easy for me to step outside my mind, which was exactly what I needed.

"Right now, all that matters is what your skin tells you. What you hear." Frey's voice was still in my ear, his breath hot on my neck.

Somehow, everything else was falling away for this moment. He had the ability to influence people's emotions, especially enhancing anything associated with passion. He could be doing that now—manipulating my reactions.

But he wouldn't. Even if I didn't know that, I

could sense it, which was an odd kind of certainty, but I trusted him regardless.

And Frey's touch felt good. His nearness was freeing.

He drew my hands back, bringing in my elbows, and hooked my fingers behind his neck.

I turned to press my cheek into his, relishing the simplicity of this moment and the heat thrumming between us. My thoughts wouldn't be held at bay for long, but I could pretend it was possible to ignore them a little longer as he gripped my hips again. This was all sway. All fluid and natural.

And every association I had with this moment was tied to me. To us. Yes, I'd learned the basics of stripping for TOM, but dancing in general, what I did when I needed to let off steam, what Frey and I were doing now, I'd gotten into for me. I did it for me. And he was the reason I'd dived deeper into the different styles. The music.

None of this was about my past.

Frey took my hand, tossed me away in a twirl, and spun me back in. My smile peeked through without my permission as he crossed my arms over my chest, leaving me hugging myself while he held me.

"How are you doing?" His question rumbled through my back.

"Real good." My answer came without hesitation.

"Ready to crank things up a smidge?"

Whatever that meant, I was up for it. "Sure."

The music slid into a thrumming rhythm that beat out *joy* with each beat. A laugh escaped without my permission as the absurdity of the moment caught up to me.

"What's so funny?" Frey's question was kind. He still spoke in that smooth, low voice that was kind and seductive and commanding all at the same time.

"This is like a scene in a movie. A stupid, fun scene that makes no sense in the real world, because ordinary people don't randomly break out in dance."

Frey dragged his nose up my neck. "This isn't random, and you're not ordinary."

A pleasant shiver spilled through me and I spun to face him. I draped my arms around his neck and pressed as closely as physics allowed. "No?"

"Definitely not." He gripped my hips and thrust against me.

This wasn't choreography. As we lost ourselves in the music it was writhing and abandon. The music spilled through me and I let it guide my body. Frey barely led, as dancing melded with desperate grinding driven by instinct.

Fen joined us, his unyielding body against my back, pressing me between them.

This was the kind of scorching safety that would burn me alive but never harm me. I tightened my grip around Frey's neck, and wrapped my legs around his waist. Fen held me up. It was impossible to tell where one of us ended and the next began.

The music stopped, and silence crashed around us.

"Guess the playlist is over," Fen growled into my shoulder.

My heart hammered against my ribs from exertion and my pulse raced with desire and anticipation. The world threatened to rush back in, and I fought to hold it back.

Fen settled his hands on my hips, and I unlocked my legs as Frey lowered me to stand on my own feet.

His gaze held mine captive, his lifetimes staring at me. I didn't know where the thought came from, but it was all there—pain, grief, love, and celebration were all reflected in his eyes. "I'm sorry I deceived you," he said softly.

There it was. The real world. "I'm sorry I've been so reactionary about... everything."

"It's a lot to take in, but you need to try."

"I'm scared." The words shredded me with truth as they tore past my lips, leaving a void and relief at the confession.

Fen leaned his forehead against the back of my skull. "You're allowed to be. I don't care what Hel or anyone else taught you."

His permission shouldn't be necessary, but it nearly made me sob.

Frey brushed his lips over mine. "We will help," he murmured. "But you have to let us."

I would've nodded, but I didn't want to break the contact. "I will, but please..." My request caught in my throat. It was the terrifying kind of weakness that should've been beaten out of me a long time ago. The kind of dependence I shouldn't have

Frey and Fen were more a part of my world than almost anyone. My list of people I never wanted to lose included them and Magnus—who was as much my sister as anyone ever would be.

"What is it?" Fen asked softly.

I swallowed hard. "Don't make me regret it."

Frey rested his forehead against mine, completing this precious, self-contained circle.

"We won't," Fen whispered into my hair.

CHAPTER 17
FREYR

I didn't realize how much Dahlia's presence, her trust, meant to me, until I thought I might lose both. Watching her seize up with doubt was heartbreaking, and I knew that was exactly what I saw.

With her reservations gone, and her being on speaking terms with me again, the rest of the day of practice went smoothly. She was confident in the dance, she added her own flair, and the finished product was a stunning sight to behold.

"Am I *good enough* to dance in your club?" Dahlia's tone was back to playful as we wrapped up the rehearsal.

I gripped her chin loosely and raised her gaze to mine. "I've never had anyone better grace my stage."

Her cheeks, already flushed from exertion,

turned a darker shade of pink, and her shy smile was worth a large fortune.

Captivating.

The peace wouldn't last long—not because of her, but because of the strife we were inviting to the front door, but tonight I wanted to enjoy the calm and I wanted Dahlia to be part of that. I dragged a thumb over her bottom lip, relishing her tiny sigh. "What do you want for dinner? Anywhere in the world."

"Pizza and Ragnarök."

I raised an eyebrow. She didn't mean the event.

"You want to order takeout and watch movies?" Fen asked.

Whoever named an action comedy after the eventual end world had a twisted sense of humor. One I was still undecided if I appreciated, though they did have a misguided sense of our history.

"Not *just* takeout," Dahlia said. "The best fucking pizza in the world. Besides..." She was in the mood to watch Hela and Loki suffer.

I fully expected that one day she'd present an edit of the movie where Fenris lived and made friends with Hulk, Loki didn't have a redemption arc, and Hela's death was much more graphic and prolonged. I offered my hand. "Let's do it."

The three of us ported back to the apartment.

"I'm going to shower real quick," Dahlia said.

Seeing her like this—carefree, relaxed... herself—was infectious. "Do you need help?"

"I *need* pizza. With extra meat." She was back to normal, without question.

I grabbed the ponytail she'd adopted halfway through the day, and tugged enough to elicit a gasp. I dragged my nose up the side of her neck to nip her ear. "Pizza now. Extra meat later."

"Bad. But also hot." She grinned and spun away toward the guest bedroom.

I ordered two meat lover's deep dish pizza from our favorite place—between Dahlia and Fen there wouldn't be leftovers. He and I moved in comfortable silence gathering plates, glasses, and beers from the kitchen and setting the table.

"I'm glad she's talking to you again." Fen's tone was low.

Me too, but the comment tugged at a thread of thought I hadn't realized was there. "It means more to you than it did a few days ago. She does."

Fen sighed. "Yes. But I think the feeling has been there longer than that. Don't ask me what it is, I don't know. She needs us. But we've never met anyone else like her. What if we need her too?"

"In what way?" I hoped he had an answer, because part of me agreed with him, but I couldn't say why.

He shrugged. "Like I said, don't ask me to define it."

"She's got a lot of growing up to do."

"She's got a little, and most mortals do."

I meet his gaze, eyebrow raised.

Fen chuckled lightly and shook his head. "How would you react if you found out you were a dragon?"

I didn't have an answer to that.

We moved back into the living room.

Dahlia emerged a short while later, her hair in twin buns. "He was right."

She shouldn't have enough hair for a Princess Leia style, and Dahlia's hair was jet black, rather than the current chestnut brown.

"Who was right?" Fen asked.

"The Tailor." Dahlia shook her head and her hair was instantly loose, tumbling freely around her shoulders and cascading down her back, ending below her ass.

Fen tugged the longer than normal locks, and she grinned.

She'd changed a portion of her appearance. Not many individuals could do that. Even shifters only had two shapes.

But Skuld had done it when they became Lance. As far as I knew, it was more of a permanent shift in forms, but it meant they had the ability.

Someone knocked.

"Pizza." Dahlia clapped, and her hair looked like

hers again, like ripping off a wig, but she hadn't touched it.

"Neat trick." Fen tugged again, and she giggled.

Without question it was good to see her back to herself. I answered the door, gave the delivery man a generic greeting, and took the food from him to set it on the table next to me. I signed the receipt, including a generous tip.

"Copper Jacket?" Shock tinged with fear lined Dahlia's question.

What?

"Goodbye, Dahlia." The pizza man knocked the clipboard from my hand as he reached inside his jacket.

The sight of a holster made my stomach churn and every muscle in my body tensed.

Fen growled.

Dahlia shouted, "*Get down.*"

Fen rushed past me as the gun went off and Dahlia screamed in pain.

Rage surged inside me, and I summoned a darker side of my ability to teleport objects. The pizza man vanished with an agonized scream of his own before Fen reached him. There were a lot of places to send someone, including a few they'd never return from.

I spun to find her on her knees, in the spot where I'd left her, a wet stain spreading across the shoulder of her black shirt. She pulled her hand away to reveal it was covered in blood.

Fuck. I should've sent her attacker someplace he'd suffer first, rather than ending his existence in a snap. Rage and worry muddied my thoughts as I knelt in front of her. "I need to see how bad the wound is."

She winced and nodded. Dealing with pain was part of her training, but that didn't mean I wanted to inflict this on her.

Fen joined us as I tore the neck of her shirt as gently as possible, and peeled the fabric away from her shoulder. Gods would burn by my hand for causing her this pain.

CHAPTER 18
DAHLIA

This was shock.

We'd learned all about it in school.

There was no pain because I was in shock.

Once that wore off, I'd be in agony. Terrified. Forced to admit that one of the few remaining Nobles had found me.

He shouldn't have missed. Even with a wolf rushing him, he should've hit me in the heart. Copper Jacket wasn't the marksman Brit was, but he had top marks with a nine-millimeter.

Frey and Fen looked so worried. This morning I would've said *serves them right*, but now I wanted to tell them it was okay. I was mortal. This was going to happen eventually.

This was like in the vision I had, in the club. Every bit of it except the surroundings. Except the club wasn't part of the vision, it was just where I happened to be when I had it.

Maybe it wasn't a real vision.

Maybe the visions weren't as literal as Artura implied.

Maybe it didn't matter because next time, my attacker wouldn't miss, and I'd be dead instead of dazed and confused.

Frey brushed his thumb over my skin and I winced in anticipation.

There was no pain.

How fucked up was my head right now?

Looking down was difficult, as my head didn't turn enough to see the spot where the bullet hit.

"There's no wound," Frey said softly. "Rather, I can see where it was, but I won't be able to much longer."

Fen tugged my shirt down farther, exposing my shoulder blade and slid his palm over my back. "Exit wound is gone too."

"I don't... What?" Now I was hallucinating.

Frey rested his clean hand against my cheek. "You were hit, but you've already healed."

"No." Because that meant... I wasn't... I grabbed the pen from where it landed when it was knocked away from Frey, and jabbed it into my bare thigh.

"*Dahlia*," Frey shouted and Fen grabbed the makeshift weapon.

I stared at the hole in my leg, watching in numb

fascination as it closed before my eye. I'd been able to change my appearance, the way The Tailor said, and now this. Artura hadn't cut me off after all?

"Is it a fluke?" I didn't know who I was asking.

Fen reached for my hand, and I offered him what should've been the injured one without thought. There was no pain when he tugged me to my feet.

"Rapid healing isn't typically like shifting," he said. "You don't summon it then send it away. Like anyone's ability to heal, at whatever rate, It's simply there."

I was looking at all the pieces to a puzzle, and they were ninety percent in place, and I still couldn't make sense of what I saw. I couldn't process. "Where did Copper Jacket go?"

"He's gone." Frey's tone implied a finality that sent shivers down my spine.

"And I'm still here."

Frey stood and dragged a thumb along my bottom lip. "If you weren't, I'd be tearing Vidar to shreds right now." The heat in his voice was familiar, but combined with his barely suppressed rage and the adrenaline coursing through me, it all sent a needy shiver through me.

"I'm still having a hard time wrapping my brain around this." Speaking the words aloud didn't help me process the situation the way I hoped. "When I was fourteen, I had a compound fracture in my arm that took more than a month to heal. I have pins in my ankle." TOM was not a friendly environment. "And now if you scratch me..."

I held my arm out, and Fen hesitated a heartbeat before dragging a claw over my skin enough to leave a faint welling of red behind. The sting was sharp and unexpectedly tantalizing.

He drew a finger over the same line, wiping away the blood to reveal there was no injury.

"That wasn't deep enough." I couldn't stop pushing the issue. What would it take for me to accept this was real? I tugged down the torn shoulder of my top, exposing the clean flesh near my collarbone.

Fen's wolf was near the surface. How did I know that? He looked human, but I felt the beast pacing inside him. Part of me wanted to join in. To shed this form and be *more*.

He sliced my skin deeply enough for me to draw in a sharp hiss that blended with his growl. He dipped his head and licked along the rapidly vanishing cut.

That shouldn't turn me on, but fuck if it wasn't hot in this moment. "Again." My request came out as a sharp whimper, and I peeled back enough of my top to expose the top of my breast.

Frey's breathing was jagged. I'd never noticed that before when he was aroused.

There were no claws this time. Fen went straight to a sharp bite that made me gasp in surprise, and followed with his rough tongue, bathing the instantly healed skin.

He moved his mouth to mine, kissing me hard as he gripped my hips and lifted.

I wrapped my arms around his neck and my legs around his waist, sinking into the primal desperation that flooded me.

Fen's growl hummed through me. "If you're not fragile, I don't have to be gentle."

My blood ran cold, and my desire vanished at the sound of his exact words from my dream. Everything about the moment was identical.

CHAPTER 19

DAHLIA

"**S**top." I pushed back, landing softly on the balls of my feet. Paranoia surged in to erase desire. From the way both men watched me, concern and confusion etched on their faces, I needed to say something. "This is too much like the other night."

Fen was working to pull himself back toward human—I sensed that in a way I didn't like.

Frey looked more contained. More rational—the very thing I'd been furious at him for yesterday. "The night you woke up screaming."

I nodded. "If that vision is real, if what I saw about TOM trying to shoot me is real, then what I saw when I attacked Fen...." I couldn't say it. My terror at the idea of doing that to anyone, but especially him, was like copper on my tongue.

"You stopped. Just now." Fen had shed his wolf. "That means the visions aren't set in stone."

"But that moment was identical. What if I can't stop next time? What if I don't have the presence of mind?" Realization struck me like a palm to the chest, knocking the air from me. "I can't stay here. I'm too much of a threat."

Frey grasped my fingers, tracing his thumb lightly over the knuckles, but also holding tight. "You need to stop and think. You're here because it's safe."

"TOM found me here. They can find me anywhere." Which I already knew. I was here because Fen and Frey were safe. Because they'd protect me. But if I killed one or both of them, it wouldn't matter, and I'd never forgive myself

Frey pulled me closer, and Fen pressed in from behind. It was similar to earlier, in the dance studio, but this time their presence didn't erase the hammering, destructive thoughts.

"We're in this with you," Frey said.

He meant to comfort me. I wanted to let him, but I couldn't. "If I'm safe, Fen's not. That's not just panic, I *know* it. The vision was so vivid."

"Dahlia." Fen tightened his grip on my hips.

No. I wouldn't let myself hurt him. Was there anywhere I could go—Tokyo, Beijing, Perth—that I was safe and so were they?

The room vanished, as did the men. What the hell?

The chatter of nearby voices washed over me, mingling with the scent of cool sand and late fall. Those were scents?

They hadn't vanished, I had. I was in Perth. At least I'd landed on a sidewalk, and on my feet, rather than in the middle of the road. Great. I was on the other side of the world, without my bag, my phone, or any money, and I was wearing sleep shorts and a torn and bloody T-shirt as a chill whipped around my bare legs and arms.

I needed to go somewhere else. Not back to Frey and Fen, as much as I ached to. Magnus was in Topeka with the Rescue Rangers, and Gwydion knew a lot about dragons. Could they help me figure out what to do next, and let the guys know I was safe in the process?

Go to Topeka. I let the thought float in my head.

I was still in Perth.

Find Magnus.

Great. Now I was treating myself like a search dog, and still not going anywhere.

"You a'ight, miss?" The accent carried on a pleasant voice.

I turned to find a woman about twice my age and a couple inches taller, studying me with concern. I'd been taught from a young age there were two options for avoiding stares in any public situation. Since I'd failed on the *blend in* front, it was time to go for *be the person everyone wants to avoid eye contact with.*

"Oh my God, can you help?" It was easy to let panic slip into my voice. I didn't even try to hide the American accent—I'd play the lost and distressed tourist. "Someone stole my purse and tore my clothes, and oh, God, it was so horrible." I let out a sob, and was tempted to give in completely to hysteria.

"Oh, darl. Come with me." She pointed me toward a nearby door. "I'm Tania. Are you here with friends or family? What's your name?"

We stepped inside a bakery, and the warm fresh scents of bread and pastries threatened to over-whelm me. Had food ever smelled so good? And why was it making it even harder to hold myself together? This entire space radiated comfort. "I'm Maggie, and no. I'm traveling alone. What am I going to do?"

Tania wouldn't have the answers I actually needed, but it was too easy to fall into this part.

She gave me a sympathetic smile. "Can you call someone in America?"

"My sister. She can wire me some money." With any luck, Magnus would wire me more than that—a ride home, a cell to lock me away from the world. Something.

"A'ight. Go wash up, and we'll take care of you."

I followed her pointing and the signs to the restroom. With the door closed and locked behind me, it was tempting to fall apart. Not an option. Not yet. Instead, I splashed cold water over my face, let the icy spray run over my hands until they were numb, and cleaned up as much of the blood on my skin as I could.

At least the shirt was black, so I didn't have to worry about stains scaring people. With a little creative maneuvering, I both tore the top more and managed to tie it so the style almost looked intentional.

When I emerged, Tania was waiting with a mug and the biggest freaking sausage roll I'd ever seen. "Sit. Have some brekkie." She nudged me toward a table half hidden by the front counter, and set everything in front of me.

I wanted to refuse, but she'd gone to all this effort. Besides, my stomach growled at the smells of coffee and pork and fresh bread. Instead, I forced myself to not eat like a total savage as I tore into the food.

While I was eating, Tania slid me a cell phone. "Call your sister."

I swallowed and managed a "Thank you" like a civilized person. I crammed the rest of my food in my mouth, washed it down with some incredible coffee, and wandered to an isolated corner of the shop to call Magnus.

"Hello?" She answered with hesitation.

"It's me."

"Where? Why? Who?"

If I wasn't so strung out, I'd smile at the terse questions. She didn't know why I was calling from an unfamiliar and foreign number, or if it was safe for me to talk. "I'm in Perth, no money or ID. It's a long story. Maybe not that long. I'd rather tell it in person."

"As in, Australia?" Magnus wouldn't ask for details like *why isn't Frey there* if they weren't offered. Not until we were face to face.

I was grateful for that. "As in."

"I don't have a way to get to you."

Right. Her ring had been destroyed. Fuck.

"But one of Kirby's boys has got to have a solution, or know someone, or something," Magnus said. "Give me fifteen minutes, and someone will find you."

"Do you need an address?" I asked.

Magnus gave a short laugh. "Don't go too far from the phone."

"I'll be waiting outside." I loved how good she was. "Oh, one more thing." I didn't want to do this, but I had to. "Promise me if Fen or Frey asks where I am, that you will tell them you don't know."

"Dahlia..."

"Long-distance pinkie swear." I couldn't let

them find me. Staying away from Fen was more important than anything.

Magnus sighed. "Long-distance pinkie swear."

I hung up, returned to the main shop, and gave Tania her phone back. "Thank you again."

She shoved a short stack of twenties into my hand.

"I can't—"

"Take it," she said. "Take care of yourself."

I thanked her again, and made a mental note of her business name. I'd be back to repay her.

Minutes ticked away far slower than minutes should be allowed to as I stood outside the bakery. Why didn't I just wait inside?

"Dahlia?" The sound of my name made my blood run cold. This was why I was outside—to keep Tania safe. No one should be addressing me by my real name here. Especially someone Magnus sent to find me.

I spun to see a woman standing far closer than I was comfortable with. Shit. She hadn't been a Noble, but she was a TOM soldier. Did they trace me here somehow or was this a coincidence?

It didn't matter. I willed myself out of here so hard I almost burst a blood vessel, but nothing happened. I needed to go anywhere else. To get the fuck out of here. To run.

She grabbed my wrist, digging her fingers into

the tendons. Sharp, painful magic crackled through me, like I'd been wrapped in a live wire.

And then I was in a room with four walls and a ceiling and nothing else.

I wouldn't let panic set in. Despite the fact it had been a long day, full of emotions that ran the gamut, and this was preferable to me turning into a dragon and ripping Fen apart. But I wouldn't lose hold of my sanity.

CHAPTER 20
FENRIR

"Where is she?" The question came out as more of a growl than I expected. Sliding from playful flirting to Dahlia being shot had wreaked havoc on my wolf, and the arousal that came after, followed by her freak out, then disappearance...

It was taking all of my restraint to confine myself to pacing. Not that I had much restraint left.

Frey shook his head. "I don't know. I can't feel her anywhere in the world. It's similar to when Artura took her."

"But Artura didn't take her." Did she? Was that possible if she wasn't in the same room as Dahlia? If it was. If Artura had—

"No," Frey said. "I think Dahlia left on her own. The energy in the room when she vanished felt similar to Artura's magic, but it tasted distinctly like Dahlia."

Rage and frustration bubbled up inside, rumbling in my chest. Artura had hidden Dahlia before, so, "If Dahlia doesn't want to be found..."

"I won't be able to find her."

"And if she's not conscious that she's doing this, or unable to get control of what she's doing?" I hated where this train of thought was leading.

Frey scrubbed his face. "I don't have any more answers than you do."

I wanted to shout at how infuriatingly calm he was, but his act was just that. He was wearing a mask to keep me from losing my shit. I loved him for it, but I hated it at the same time. "I can't sit here and do nothing. Neither can you."

"No." Frey sighed. "But doing a random thing for the sake of acting won't accomplish anything, and it will have us distracted if a solution pops up."

I roared and swung at the nearest target, putting my fist through the wall. The bruises, broken skin, and cracked knuckles healed instantly, and I was tempted to do it again so I'd have the pain to distract me.

"I'll call Artura, in case I'm wrong," Frey said.

I was grateful for the concession, and surprised she took his call. The terse conversation didn't yield any results, though. I knew it even before he disconnected.

"Call Magnus," I said. "If Dahlia did this on her own, or if she's contacted anyone, it will be Magnus." Forcing myself to think was infuriating because it forced me to stay human.

Frey did as I said, and while his half of the conversation was more pleasant than the previous one, he didn't have any more luck.

This was thirty-one flavors of wrong. We didn't know if she was missing because she chose it or because she'd been taken. On the off chance she was safe now, she wouldn't be for long. "What now?"

"We'll call in favors. Magnus said she and the Rescue Rangers would let us know if they saw anything. We'll ask everyone everywhere to put eyes and ears out."

That sounded great, with one small exception. "We don't have a lot of allies left to call in those favors with."

"No, we don't." Frey shook his head. "So it's time to grovel." He was already dialing and putting the phone to his ear. "It's me. We need to talk."

I put a leash on my wolf and grabbed my phone as well. My contact list was short, and the number of those who would take my call was even fewer, but I was going to dial every one of them anyway. I was about three quarters of the way through, with only a few offers of help, when I smelled a new person in the air.

Aya had appeared in the middle of the living room. "You summoned me?"

"You were right." Frey's voice was as tight as the clench of his jaw.

His resignation cut deep, but the underlying hint of his rage fed mine.

"Hmm." Aya frowned. "What do you want?"

"Dahlia's missing. I need your resources to help find her," Frey said.

Aya nodded. She'd kept up with technology, and like Frey had embraced the modern era. As a goddess of war, she understood that these days as many battles were fought through digital subterfuge as in person. "Yes. I won't ask anything in return since it's for her."

"But you want something." I was aware of what she wanted from Frey—to join the fight. He'd held off at least in part because of me, but I wasn't interested in restraint anymore. I wanted a fight.

"I do, but I won't trade your help for her life. Not after what she did for me," Aya said.

Noble of her. "You'll have whatever you need from us regardless." I spoke before Frey could. "Once we have Dahlia back and she's safe, ask whatever you will of me."

Aya pursed her lips. "I'll put feelers out, far and wide. As long as she's not the one hiding herself, if any traces of her show up online, I'll find them."

That exception was the bit that had me concerned.

Aya blinked from the room with a curt nod.

I was tempted to ask Frey to teleport us to random spots around the world, cities Dahlia had mentioned in the past, on the off chance we'd find her in one. The odds were supremely low, but they were higher than if we stayed here, sitting on our hands.

Frey's phone rang and he put it on speaker. "Yes?"

"Dahlia is missing." Magnus's voice was hollow and tinny coming from the small speaker.

I snarled. "We know. That's why—" *Fuck.* "You lied to Frey. You knew where she was." My anger cranked higher. Magnus was lucky she wasn't here.

"Dahlia made me promise not to tell you that I'd talked to her, and I can't break a promise to her."

I wanted to argue, but then I'd lose control, and I needed answers more. "How do you know she's missing now?"

"Min sent a contact to meet her, and she wasn't there. She wasn't anywhere. I checked security cameras in the area, and she ran into a former class-mate then they both vanished."

Frey covered my fist with his hand and held my gaze. It wasn't comfort that flowed between us, but an understanding that someone would suffer for this.

"You need to send us a list of every TOM location you know of," Frey said.

"It won't matter, but okay," Magnus agreed. "Give me five minutes and you'll have the most recent intel I have on everything."

Frey disconnected and tossed the phone onto the couch. "You staying with me?" He held my gaze.

"For now." I'd save the *losing my shit* part of this until we had Dahlia back, and then all bets were off.

CHAPTER 21

DAHLIA

I was going to will myself out of here. I'd teleported to Perth, I'd broken Artura's shield that kept Frey from finding me, and now I was going to harness this fucking dragon of mine and make it work for me.

My senses picked up everything, from the hum of hidden fans to the scent of stone and sweat to the slowly rising chill in the air. If this was anything like other facilities, and I had no reason to believe it wouldn't be, TOM would make me more and more uncomfortable, rather than outright torture me.

Though, why they hadn't outright killed me was beyond me.

I settled in the middle of the room and tried to turn my focus inward, despite the external threat.

There was someone else in here with me who wore a faint perfume and had a racing pulse.

"Hi, Dahlia."

Minato. Betrayal spilled inside, and I hid the reaction. "Did they get you too?" I asked as I faced her. As much as I hated the thought, I wanted it to be true that she was here because she'd been captured by TOM and not because she'd betrayed me.

"Yes, but no. They got me months ago."

But I'd seen her at the club recently. Interacted with her. Danced with her. "Have you been here the whole time?" I knew the answer, but the same part of me that saved her life instead of assassinating her refused to believe she'd turn on me.

Minato shook her head. "When they send you to kill a potential, do they tell you which prophecies relate to us? Did they tell you who I was supposed to become?"

"No."

"I'm a baku."

"An idiot?"

Minato scowled. "That's a baka. I feed on dreams. Do you know what your people do when their target goes missing?"

I could correct her and tell her if they were still my people, I wouldn't be in this cell, but that wasn't the point. "Yes." TOM hunted down everyone associated with a potential in an effort to drag their target out of hiding. Very few potentials survived that long, but for those FU rescued, more than just the target had to be given a new life. And I'd erased any and all paper trails leading to Minato's old life when I walked away from the mission to destroy her.

"You're lucky they found you, brought you here, before they decided to go after your loved ones. Magnus isn't hiding at all, and Freyr and Fenrir..."

"They took you in. Hid you. Kept you safe." As my frustration and anger grew, I felt the familiar prickles of scales and wings pressing against my skin.

Minato frowned. "My brother is all I have left, and he has so much potential. Even if I never see him again, as long as he survives this, that's the only thing that matters to me. You understand, don't you?"

I didn't want to. "If you're dead, he shouldn't have to worry." My threat carried on a gravel voice that bled into a language I didn't recognize. My claws and tail appeared as I lunged, but Minato was already gone.

Here was my dragon—my other half. I was whole. I let the power and rage and grace and wisdom of the beast spill through me, as a screeching yowl ripped from my chest and echoed in my cage.

This room couldn't hold me. I felt the knowledge I needed to leave this place, to blink away and never return, but I was going to leave my mark on this base while I was here. Ensure those who came after never forgot the little girl they used to spit on and mock.

My transformation rolled over my entire body. I didn't need a mirror to know I was a full-blown dragon now, but I was still tiny. I needed to be bigger. Uncontainable.

As my form grew, it pressed into the walls and ceiling, and the structure pressed back, threatening to squash my spirit. Never again. I pushed back until I felt cracks form, then the walls and ceiling crumbled around me. *Freedom*. I flew straight up, forcing my way through concrete and steel with barely a cringe, earth falling in around me and filling the hole I left behind.

Then I was above ground, sunlight streaming around me and bouncing off the sand. Underground base in the middle of the desert? If I dove back down as a dragon would I do as much damage as I did coming up? I hoped so.

The familiar sound of gunfire greeted me, and bullets bounced off my skin. I would destroy them all. They'd never do anything like this to another person again.

CHAPTER 22
FREYR

The list Magnus provided had thousands of locations, including safe houses and establishments that were TOM friendly. Even if I eliminated everything but known training bases and larger locations, there were hundreds. I wasn't going to waste our time hopping from place to place to place in the hopes she may or may not be there.

I couldn't just sit here anymore than Fen could, waiting for Aya or someone else to come back with information.

A thought bounced in my head, and I reached for it. It flitted away before I grasped and yanked. When I called Artura, she'd answered with *I'm not the one who has her*. Before I asked. Before I said anything. And she'd answered on the first ring, despite it being the middle of the night where she was.

Fuck me. I wanted this to be an in-person visit. I rested a hand on Fen's shoulder, stopping his pacing. "Let's go," I said, and phased us without further fanfare.

We landed on the street in front of *The Dragon's Hoarde*. It was barely four in the morning, and there were very few people. The shop wasn't open, and I didn't expect it to be.

Recognition and understanding flashed on Fen's face as we headed to the back of the building, to a small door. I wasn't surprised when Artura answered before I finished knocking.

"We're sorry to disturb you at this early hour." I gave a short bow.

I wanted to make immediate demands, but despite her intrusions in my home and our desperation, centuries of propriety kept me from doing so. I was also willing to beg to get her help.

Her expression was bland. "I believe I made it clear I was done with everything surrounding Dahlia."

"You know where she is." Fen's statement was barely controlled anger.

Artura shook her head. "I don't."

"You knew I would call, you knew she was taken, and you knew we'd show up here this evening," I said.

"I did, and that is the extent of my knowledge.

Have a good morning, gentlemen." She moved back to swing the door shut.

I stepped inside, keeping her from closing us out. Fuck propriety. She'd come into NEON once without permission and once attacking my guests. She was lording her power and knowledge over us like... like a fucking god, and no one was going to stand in our way. "You're going to help us find Dahlia."

"And why, dear child, would I do that?" Condescension spilled into her question. "For honor? For family? Because it's the right thing to do?"

"No." The answer came to me quickly because it had been my excuse for so long. I realized I was wrong, but Artura would have to arrive at that conclusion for herself. "Because you're tired. Because you don't want to be involved with humanity as a whole, and Dahlia could take that burden from you. Because for whatever unknown reason, fates outside even your grasp have decided that there should be three of you, and if you let her perish, the odds your next ascended niece or nephew will be anything even near as incredible as her are non-existent."

Was I biased when it came to Dahlia? Yes. I was also right. "Because your visions said you would help."

"They didn't." Artura stepped aside and gestured for us to enter. "I no longer see anything around Dahlia."

Fen growled and my heart sank. But no visions didn't mean Dahlia's death. "You didn't see anything around Skuld in the end, either."

"It's true." Artura led us through the back of the shop to a small sitting room. The one I'd found Dahlia in last time I came here. "I didn't realize you'd be staying, or I would have had coffee and biscuits ready. I apologize." She gestured for us to sit.

"Must be awkward for you. Not knowing something." Fen stayed near the door.

She raised her brows. "It is not as unusual as you think. We're not omniscient—we don't see everything. Only specific moments of significance in time."

"Did you tell Dahlia that?" Fen asked.

Artura shrugged. "She'll figure it out. I told her what mattered—that what we see is never wrong."

"So if she saw herself tearing me to shreds..." Fen let the thought hang.

"She will."

"Will he survive?" Perhaps that was an ignorant thing for me to ask.

Artura folded her hands in her lap. "Presumably not, if he's torn apart. I wonder what part of *I don't see anything else around Dahlia* you don't understand. I'm not a fortune teller. I have dreams, they show me out of context snippets of time. It's the same for Urd, it was the same for Skuld. I assume it's the same for Dahlia."

This was ridiculous. I wouldn't sit here for hours, or even minutes more, waiting for Artura to offer up a snippet of useful information. "What do you know that will help us? I don't want a vague response. I don't want anything held back. Tell me."

"I don't—"

"*Now*." Fen's roar echoed off the walls and shook my soul, as his aura grew to consume the room.

Artura actually looked startled. "Her sister, the auburn-haired Valkyrie, knows a god."

Magnus? "She knows several of them," I said.

"A god who sits on the board of The Order of Mistletoe. Yes, I realize she's met several of those, too. A quorum of assholes who can't accept their days are numbered. She's friends with this one."

No she wasn't. Magnus left that entire life behind. "And?"

"And nothing." Artura started back. "I don't know anymore. There are hints that he may brush Dahlia's future, because my visions with him distort and fade."

"Great." It was a starting point. "So we'll track down Vidar."

"Not that one." Artura shook her head.

Was she making this difficult on purpose? No wonder there were so many ways to interpret the prophecies. "Which one?"

"I don't know the name of every face that passes through my mind."

I wanted to call this a waste of time, but we had more information than before. Not much, but it was a starting point. "Thank you for your time."

"I do hope you find her," Artura said. "I'll see you out."

As we headed to the rear of the shop again, my phone rang. My pulse quickened—news about Dahlia? "I need to take this, I apologize." We paused halfway to the exit as I answered the phone.

"I know where your girl is."

I frowned at the greeting and the almost musical voice. "Bragi?" Not someone I had called. In fact, he was one of the last people I expected to hear from, since he sat on the TOM board.

"She's in Saint Moritz."

This wasn't right. "Switzerland? Why are you giving me this?" It was true, a large number of the gods disliked my apparent neutrality—perhaps that was why he thought the location was humorous— but they hadn't pursued us directly before now.

"So you can go get your girl."

"Or you could bring her here." I'd be gone in an instant if I believed anything he was saying.

Bragi sighed. "Our soldiers aren't the only ones who have become disenchanted with TOM's trajectory. However, I'm not ready to tip my hand yet, and freeing her does that."

"Why would I trust you?"

"Such a fucking cliché. You wouldn't. But if you

want her, you'll find her in Saint Moritz." Bragi disconnected.

He was right—the entire exchange was a cliché. Did I walk into the trap, hoping Dahlia was there, or risk abandoning her?

CHAPTER 23

FENRIR

I inferred a lot from Freyr's half of the conversation.

"Do we believe him?" I asked the instant he hung up. The answer was *no*, but Frey would catch the underlying meaning. Was there anything Bragi said that was worth listening to?

Frey shook his head. "I don't know. I don't remember Saint Moritz being on the list from Magnus."

There was no reason TOM wouldn't have new or additional locations. Something tickled my thoughts and I reached for it. "That was Bragi."

Frey stared back, expression bland. "Yes."

"A god from TOM whom Magnus is—was— friendly with." I was trying to contain myself. We needed to vet this information, but my wolf was roaring to be loosed.

"It's a tenuous thread."

"If I may." Artura's voice startled me.

How did I forget she was here? In her own home?

Because I had more important things to worry about than a dragon who ran out of fucks centuries ago. "By all means."

"The location Bragi gave you. Can you sense it? Can you sense Dahlia there?" Artura asked.

A reasonable question and a good indicator that the longer we waited, the less clearly I was thinking. This was battle. War. The screams of my enemies—

"I can't." Frey's response kept me grounded.

For now.

Artura's forehead wrinkled and she closed her eyes. After a moment, she focused on us again. "There's a structure there, under the mountains, that's not on this plane. It's been taken out of this world and resides in a small pocket of the Fae world, using the same magic Magnus had access to. Would Bragi send you to a place you can't reach?"

"Not as a trap, no." Frey's answer summoned more of my insistence.

"Let's go. Bring Magnus maybe, in case she's familiar with the layout. Kirby. Anyone who's willing." I wanted to pace. I wanted to shift. Neither was practical in this small space, but as soon as we got to this new location...

Frey rested a hand on my chest, over my heart. "You can't go with me. I don't give a fuck if you lose control, but you're the one person I won't sacrifice to get her back."

His touch both soothed and ignited. "That's not your decision."

"But I do have a say. After all this time, I have a right to ask you not to do this." Frey's piercing gaze met mine.

I covered his hand and squeezed gently as a strange calm snaked through me. This wasn't the kind of peace that said *walk away*, it was a feeling that had been there for as long as I remembered, that assured me this fight was the right one for me to be in. "I understand, but this isn't the suicide mission for me that you think it is."

"But you would sacrifice yourself for Dahlia." Frey's tone was hard to read.

"I'd sacrifice myself for you. But when it comes to her, I'm not worried about her hurting me." I didn't care about visions or prophecies or the power of beings older than the gods. Only two beings in this world deserved my faith—Freyr and Dahlia. "When I go, millennia down the line, she won't be the cause."

Frey nodded. "When this is over, when she's safe, the three of us will talk about where she fits with us."

"We will." I kissed his knuckles.

"I can take you to Saint Moritz," Artura said. "I'll fight with you to get her back."

I stared at her in disbelief. "Is this funny to you? Is your sense of humor so warped that an offer like that amuses you?"

Her smile didn't reach her eyes. "I'm tired. Not tonight, but in general. I've seen the worst humanity has to offer. Not just the isolated incidents, but all of it has haunted my dreams since before I knew what a human was. The visions rarely show us warm and safe images. However, every once in a while I meet someone who makes the world feel less draining. You, fierce wolf, are not one of those people. But your loyalty gives me hope, and Dahlia is one of those people.

"Frey is right. I'm lucky this gift or curse or destiny or whatever it is fell to Dahlia. It would be lovely if she could keep being disillusioned for at least a few centuries, and the two of you will help with that. As for her vision about Fen, I had visions thousands of years ago that are only coming true now. Dahlia won't rip you to shreds tomorrow, and when she does, she and Frey will have each other."

"You fail to understand how much Fen means to me." The rumble in Frey's voice was low and threatening.

Artura never flinched. "Things change."

"Fuck, you really are jaded." I didn't care, as long as she didn't turn on us. "What do we need, in order to do this?" The answer needed to be *we're set, let's go.*

"An idea of what we're walking into would be nice," Frey said. "Manpower. Magnus's familiarity with TOM thinking. Starkad's."

I bit off a growl. I didn't like Starkad any more than Dahlia did, but he could be a valuable ally. These days. And he'd been with TOM longer than the soldiers like Dahlia and Magnus, so he had a good idea of how they thought. "Call her."

While he dialed, I gave Artura a brief nod, and stepped outside to burn off some energy. The alley wasn't big enough for much, but it let me pace and condense my drive into a focused ball of momentum. Should I be dreading a fight? I felt like Frey would want me to, but I was looking forward to another good battle.

Frey's hand on my arm paused me, and I realized he had Magnus with him. I'd been so lost in my thoughts I hadn't noticed him leave.

"No one else is available," she said.

I didn't care. "We'll be enough." It wasn't as though we were taking on a dragon, and we would have one by our side. "What do we need to know."

Magnus gave us a quick rundown of what to expect, which drilled down to we should expect well trained and armed guards, cameras, and no entry point left unmonitored.

I was fine with that. We were all bulletproof in our own ways, and even the most disciplined soldier frequently turned and ran at the sight of a wolf the size of a truck bearing down on them.

Artura took a deep breath and straightened to full height. She was the most imposing one and a half meter tall individual I'd ever met. "I can't break their spell from here, but once we're there, I can shatter the magic enough to give us a doorway in. Are you ready?"

"Yes." More than ready.

Our environment shifted and the temperature dropped enough for the chill to gnaw at my bones. Wind and snow whipped around us, and the space in front of us turned to a glassy looking rectangle.

I growled as I finally let the wolf free.

CHAPTER 24

DAHLIA

Destroy. Vengeance. Escape. Freedom.

The faceless soldiers were irritations. Guns that fired pellets that bounced off my scales. Why were they trying?

For each that fired, I fought back. For each I destroyed, they vanished, another taking their place.

The sun was blinding. The sand hot.

Why was I so cold? Why didn't any of these people, these men, and women I'd grown up with, have faces? Why was I killing them when so many of them didn't have any more choice to be here than I'd had?

They were attacking me.

They weren't hurting me though.

They'd locked me away.

I was free now, and could leave.

They would follow.

A chill raced over me and I shuddered. I wanted to tuck myself into a little ball and warm up, but that didn't make any sense in this sunshine.

Nothing about this was right—the setting, the mindset, the tiny nagging voice trying to fill in pieces in my mind. Memories of how I'd gotten here. What came before.

This was like a bad dream and I wanted to wake up.

I was in a room with four walls and a ceiling. Nothing else. I was human again. No, someone else was here with me. Minato sat with her back to the wall, knees to her chest, shivering, with tears streaked down her cheeks.

It was fucking cold in here. Why was it so cold in the middle of the desert?

"I want to leave." Minato's voice shook. "Can you get us out?"

I didn't trust her. Why not? Why couldn't I remember. Something about dreams—

"Please." Minato reached for me. "You know how hard it is to get away from them. Neither of us wants to be here."

She was wearing the same dress she'd danced in, that night at...

Why couldn't I remember? There was a blank void in my head before now. Before... What?

No, Minato was wearing the same outfit she had been when I met her. Denim skirt. Backpack.

She looked so young. My mind was too fragmented.

"You can get us out of here," she said.

Could I? In a room with no doors or windows? How did we get in here? Wait, I knew how to do something. "Because I'm a dragon." That wasn't right. My dragon didn't obey me. I was a dragon?

Minato shook her head. "Because you're you."

"That doesn't make any sense." None of this does.

"Please. They have my brother. They're going to kill him." Tears welled in Minato's eyes.

There it was. I reached for the thought, but I could only grasp a single word. "Baku."

"Yes. That's me. I'm a baku."

Son of a... My mind, my memories, flitted back in. Thoughts began to line up. I'd been with Frey and Fen. I ran away to keep from hurting them. TOM found me. I shifted—full-on shifted into a dragon. But now I was human again.

Because this wasn't real. "I've loved all things magic since before I was old enough to understand what I was watching," I said.

Minato's tears vanished behind her frown. "Okay?"

"Buffy, Supernatural, The Magicians... I've watched them all more times than I can count."

Minato gave me a tentative smile. "Will that help you get us out of here?"

Fuck. She had me trapped in a dream. "Can they see what you're seeing, or do you have to tell them, once you're done with me?"

"I don't understand." The emotion was gone from Minato's voice.

"Or do you stick me in a loop until I do whatever you want in real life, because I've lost all sense of reality?"

Minato stared back.

At least she was done with the leading questions. "Come on. If you were going to trap me in a TV trope, why did it have to be the one I hate? Why couldn't this be the episode where everyone is horny and can't stop fucking? I suppose I should be glad you didn't build us a mental institute and try to convince me I was crazy and the gods aren't real."

"The gods never want to convince people not to believe in them, you know that." Minato stood and stretched her back. "Besides, you don't have a fear of mental institutes."

"No shit. Am I even talking to you , or are you a projection of my subconscious?"

"This is me."

Maybe it was, maybe it wasn't. "My subconscious might say that."

"No, it wouldn't, or I wouldn't need to be here." Minato shook her head. "Fen dreads the day he can't protect you or Frey—that's his biggest nightmare, did you know that? He's scared he'll forget himself and lose one of you in the process. Frey is terrified of something similar—that he'll find himself impotent when he's needed most."

Minato gave a strained chuckle. "But you. The soldiers had bets about what your biggest fear was —losing your intelligence or being forced to return to TOM. But no, not Dahlia. My touch should have set you in a nightmare that gave them exactly what they needed, without me nudging. The one piece of information that would set my brother free."

"Oh. My. God. Are you evil villain monologuing? People do that?" I wanted answers, but I also wanted to irritate her. See if she would slip. "You stuck me in a dream so you could read me a speech?"

"I stuck you in a dream because TOM expected you to react a certain way and you didn't. Now I'm in control, because apparently, unlike anyone else in the known universe, your deepest darkest nightmare is becoming one of the most powerful creatures in existence and destroying everything without care. So now, we'll talk, I'll figure out what to do next, and try again."

Un-fucking-believable. "That's not the way this trope works, though. You're supposed to drive me nuts and then I'll confess anything."

"This isn't a TV show, Dahlia. There's no fade to black at the end of forty-five minutes." Minato raked her fingers through her hair. "Why didn't you just assassinate me, back then, like you were supposed to?"

Was the question part of the manipulation? I didn't think so. "Because killing you wasn't right."

"And this is somehow better?"

"I didn't know this was coming, and I can't live my life in fear of what comes next." I'd always believed that. "I have to make the best decisions I can at the time with the information I have." The words tugged a thought in the back of my mind, about my visions, but the revelation vanished in a blink before I could grab it.

"Stay out of your conscious mind, I need you in here," Minato snapped. "I need you focused on me and the dream. *Fuck.* You're supposed to be thinking you're helping me escape."

"What kind of information does that get you?" I couldn't figure it out. I'd escaped as a dragon, but she needed to be with me for some reason. Her intentions didn't make sense.

"Fuck this. I need you less aware."

That meant she was going to push me back toward dragon dreams, where it was hard to grasp my own thoughts. How did I know that? I just did, and I didn't want to go back to that state of mind. "You could just ask me what you want to know. I'm here for information, aren't I? Or they would have killed me. Or kept torturing me."

"Tell me how to bypass the Huldra Protocol

without triggering Hydra, and without using forced insertion, while still salvaging the python script that drives the ETL subroutine."

I understood individual components of her question, but pieced into a single sentence, the words made less sense than anything else here. "What?"

Minato sighed. "Only your subconscious knows the answer; the information is buried deep under your sense of reality. So I need to strip your reason away. I'm sorry, Dahlia, I really am, but either you give them what they want, or they trap you here in this cell, in this dream, forever. They won't let you run free, knowing how to stop them."

But I didn't know how to stop them.

I was rushing toward Minato again, despite not wanting to, my scales and wings growing in. Rage took over as my dragon form grew larger than the cell.

Where was I? Why was this happening? I'd just been talking to... someone? I had to hold onto my thoughts. This wasn't real.

But it felt like it. It felt so very real.

CHAPTER 25
FREYR

We were a terrifying group. When Fen was in his full wolf form, he was as large as a truck.

Magnus's wings were the same deep auburn as her hair, and her armor was detailed with skulls for pauldrons and an intricate leaf and vine pattern covering the breastplate. It was meant to intimidate more than be practical, since she was bulletproof without it.

Artura's skin was white and violet scales, her tail snaked around her leg, and her wings rivaled Magnus's in size. She'd stayed humanoid, but she was twice as tall as usual.

My physical appearance didn't change. My aura did. I may have been a god of sex and fertility, but I'd learned a lot having a twin who was a goddess of war, and the visible glow around me would make most sane people think twice about fucking with me.

We stepped through the gate, and Artura hissed. "This entire place uses the same magic that created Magnus's ring. It's littered with pieces of Skuld and fae blood. I can't get rid of it without destroying everything."

"Soon enough." The thought of what it took to build a structure like this made me ill. The magic itself would also keep me from doing to anyone else what I'd done to the assassin at our apartment, but there were other ways to make someone suffer.

Fen paused and sniffed the air. *"Dahlia's here."* Without human vocal cords, he didn't speak in the normal way—his voice was more like an echo in my thoughts.

With one set of doors behind us, where we'd stepped through the gate, and another in front of us, there was only one direction to go, so we went forward.

Magnus kicked the doors open, and the sound drew the attention of three guards sitting at what looked like a check in station.

The first soldier opened fire before we cleared the room. Bullets sliced through walls and us, wounds healing instantly.

Fen lunged for the gunmen and a second leaned on his trigger as well.

"Magnus?" The third stepped back, gun hanging limply at his side.

Fen made quick work of his target. With a flick of my wrist, I broke the neck of the second. An eerie still settled over the room, leaving a ringing in my ears.

The surviving soldier stopped when his back it a wall. "I heard you'd changed, but—"

"We don't have time," I said.

Magnus held up a finger, and approached the soldier. "It's okay." She covered his hand and his gun hit the floor hard. "I know who you really are, even if TOM never did." A dagger appeared in her hand. "You're worthy. Valhalla awaits." She drove the knife through his gut.

I swallowed a gasp at the potency of the moment. At seeing someone new practice the old ways.

"You can't do that with everyone." Artura didn't sound impressed.

Magnus shrugged. "You have your rituals, I have mine. I'll do it when it's appropriate."

Artura rolled her eyes. "Step back."

The steel wall and door in front of Magnus glowed red then white as it liquefied, and backpedaled quickly away from the puddle of molten metal.

I couldn't do fire, but I could do ice. I cooled the pool in an instant, letting the ice crackle and sizzle with pockmarks so we could walk over a fresh textured surface.

Magnus led the way. "Assume every corner is a trap."

"*Of course*," Fen said.

No gunfire greeted us as we moved into the new room. There were no corners, either. Instead a long hall stretched out in front of us, dotted with the occasional door.

Magnus pressed a finger to her lips, pointed at me, pointed to the door on the left, and held up her hand.

She gestured to Fen, and indicated the door across from my assignment. She held up three fingers, folded them down one at a time, and kicked through the second door on *one*. As she moved in to sweep the room, I kept an eye on the rest of the hallway.

I was a little surprised Artura didn't disrupt the instructions or take her own route.

The first room was empty. We repeated the process all the way down the hall, and didn't encounter a single soul.

"*Where is everyone?*" Fen asked. "*This place smells occupied.*"

People had been here, but they left recently. As in, moments ago. I felt the charge of magic in the air.

"There aren't many of them left," Magnus said.

"Not of those we went to school with. This may have been a matter of preserving numbers."

If that was the case, "Is Dahlia here still?"

Fen growled. "*Yes.*"

There were no more doors, though. "Where?"

"Here." Artura pressed her hand to the blank wall in front of us.

As with before, the wall glowed white-hot and melted into a puddle.

Dahlia lay on the other side, on the ground, in the middle of a vast cavern. The room must have been as big as the rest of the building.

A faint glow circled her, ebbing in rhythm with her breathing. "Magic is keeping her asleep. But it's not strong."

I approached, relief spilling through me that she was okay. That the spell of song encasing her would be easy to break. I rested a hand on her shoulder, and shattered the sleep.

Dahlia's eyes shot open, and she looked directly at me. "You've got to be fucking kidding me. You little bitch." Venom and rage dripped from her voice.

"Dahlia, it's me." I kept my voice even, and dropped the aura of terror.

"Sure." Dahlia hopped to her feet, sund landed more than a meter from us. "I mean, obviously it's *you*. Because I haven't seen *you* yet." She turned her gaze to the ceiling. "I'm so sick of this," she screamed.

"It is us." Magnus approached slowly. "Do you remember—"

"Nuh-uh." Dahlia shook her head. "Whatever you're about to say is bullshit. Of course I remember. We're in my head, you fucking cunt."

Magnus scoffed. "Excuse me, bitch?"

This didn't make sense. What did we walk into?

"Oh, and she even talks like Magnus. *Where the fuck are you?*" Dahlia's shout shook the walls, and her scales slid in. Her tail and wings followed, until her form resembled Artura's.

She could have picked a less convenient time to learn to control her power, but not much. I couldn't put the pieces together, but she needed to calm down. "It really is us," I said.

"Like they're going to tell me anything else? They're not going to say *you got us, we're part of the dream.* You fucked up though." Dahlia wasn't looking at us.

A shield appeared in Magnus's hand and sword in the other. "I've never said this before, but you've lost it."

Dahlia laughed and shook her head. "I knew you'd get it wrong sooner or later. Artura would never come for me. She doesn't give a shit who I am or what I do." Dahlia's human form vanished, and a dragon the size of a small house stood in front of us. She wasn't large enough to fill the room, but she certainly dominated it.

"*We won't hurt you,*" Fen said.

Magnus's laugh was strained. "Do you remember dragons? We *can't* hurt her."

"I can." Artura was instantly a dragon as well. Black standing against white. Power flickering through the room.

"Stay inside the shield," Magnus said.

Fen sprinted away, placing himself between Artura and Dahlia.

No. This wasn't happening. If I couldn't teleport Fen back to our plane, could I send him someplace in the Fae realm? Would that be any more dangerous than him being caught in the crossfire?

I didn't know, but this wouldn't be the day Fen died, and I didn't want today to be the day I made a choice beyond that.

For the first time in my existence, I understood why people prayed.

CHAPTER 26

DAHLIA

I lost track of how many scenes I was forced through, and those were just the ones I was aware of. I was certain that Minato forced me through at least as many before I grasped enough control of my consciousness to remember who and where I was from dream to dream.

Every so often she'd pop back in to see if I'd lost my mind yet, but I'd figured out how to keep her out. Or I thought I had. I wasn't waking up, and this dream was some seriously fucked up bullshit, so maybe she'd found her way back in.

Magnus was in this dream, along with Frey, Fen, and Artura of all people. I had no idea why Minato thought that was a good idea.

Though, given that Artura was currently a dragon—an ancient, powerful, terrifying dragon—

facing down my newbie dragon self, maybe I'd come up with this new nightmare on my own.

If this was another of Minato's stupid fucking dreams, I was ending it. We were in my head and I was taking control, so we could move on to her next attempt to traumatize me.

Artura-dragon stepped closer, an earth-rattling roar tearing from her throat.

I screeched back. At least I sounded impressive with a dragon.

And then my brain ground to a halt as what I saw overlapped with what I'd seen in visions. Fen staring me down, standing between me and shapes that had only been shadows before, but made sense now. A low growl rumbled through the room, emanating from him, and he bared his teeth.

I reared up with a roar, exposing my own fangs, and extending my claws.

"*Stop*." Fen's voice was in my head, calm rather than harsh. His posture changed in a blink, and he sank back on his haunches. "*I won't hurt you*."

This wasn't right. It wasn't like my vision. What kind of games was Minato playing now?

My mind faltered as Fen became human before my eyes. The vision wasn't happening. Like with the sex, things were playing out differently. And like with the sex, this felt real. There was no disconnect between my thoughts and my body and my memories.

I let my dragon form vanish, and stared at him, waiting for something to be wrong. "Are you real?" I felt stupid for asking. No one had said *no* yet, through every bullshit dream Minato had fed me.

Fen nodded.

"How do I know?" I was asking myself as much as I was him or anyone else in the room.

He grasped my fingertips loosely and a shock raced through me at the contact. At how solid and real he felt. He brushed his thumb over the back of my knuckles. None of those fucking dreams came with this kind of tactile sensation.

"The same way you know anything; you trust yourself." Fen slid his hand to the back of my neck, pulled me in, and brushed his lips over mine.

My mouth fell open in a silent gasp at the solidness of his touch, and his tongue slipped in to dance with mine. I could taste him. Smell him. Hear the heavy hammer of his pulse and the way it beat out a rhythm with mine.

This kiss wasn't the stuff of nightmares of fevered, induced dreams. It was real. He was solid. Which meant everyone else in the room was real too, and I couldn't shrug off the world in favor of staying wrapped in comfort.

Fen pressed his forehead to mine, still holding me in place. "Are you with us again?"

I nodded, but not so much I broke the contact. A new thought occurred to me. "It didn't happen."

When I thought I was trapped in the dream, the news didn't matter.

"What didn't?"

"My vision didn't come true. I didn't kill you."

Frey's exhale was soft, but I heard it as if it was loud enough to bounce off the ceiling a dozen meters above.

"It was just like my vision. Every single second." The images were still fresh in my mind, both real and foretold in my visions, and they overlapped in every detail, until the instant Fen dropped his wolf form. "Except, it didn't come true."

Fen squeezed my hand. "I knew you wouldn't, Duckie."

Artura sighed quietly, but her irritation was tangible. I wanted to ask why she was even here, but we were still in the middle of enemy territory. I stepped back so I could see everyone, and focused on Magnus. "I wasn't calling *you* a cunt."

She rolled her eyes, a smile threatening. "Whatever. Thanks for not killing us."

"It's the least I could do." I shrugged. "What are we looking at?"

"Nothing. Seriously." Magnus gestured to a hole in the wall that looked like it had been smelted into place. "What you see behind us is it."

An empty hallway? I knew Vidar wasn't the most creative asshole, but this was weak even for him. It also couldn't be right because Minato wanted me to help her escape, and there had to be a reason for that. Or was that all meant to be a metaphorical thing, in my mind? "There has to be more here."

Magnus shook her head. "Whole lotta nothing and no one."

That wasn't right. In fact, none of what I saw on the other side of the wall was right. Not in that *I'm still trapped in Minato's stupid dream* kind of way, but there was more to the building.

Wait. "I can feel buildings now? Is that... a dragon thing?" I looked at Artura, like I was actually going to get an answer. Why was she here?

"No," she said. "At least, not in the way you're thinking. You feel the building because the entire structure was built the same way Magnus's ring was created."

We were walking around in dragon parts and tortured fae? A shudder spilled down my spine. "That's some dark shit." But Minato had wanted me to find something. Do *something*. None of this made sense.

If we found her, we could make her tell us. But as I extended my senses—how did I know to do that?— I didn't feel any other life here besides the people in this room. That was a creepy trick.

"Where is everyone?" I asked.

"There weren't many people here." Frey's speaking caught me off-guard, and the way he studied me made me uneasy. "Three. Gone now."

Gone as in *dead*. "Minato?"

Frey frowned. "What?"

Right. They were as lost about what I'd been through as I was about their arrival. "She sold me out to TOM. Supposedly to protect her brother. She had me trapped here." We didn't have time for talking. The building may be empty now, but that didn't mean it would stay that way. "I can explain later. All of it. Was Minato one of the three?"

"She's not here." Fen sniffed the air. "I don't know if she ever was. We need to go."

Fuck. I had so many questions, and most of them wouldn't be answered by this group. I gestured down the hallway. "Through the third door on the left, other side of the wall. We need to be there, first."

Despite everyone agreeing the place was empty, we proceeded with caution. The main room held an uncomfortable charge that made my skin crawl, but I managed to shrug off the sensation. If human beings had occupied this place, it didn't make sense that important rooms were only accessible magically.

I tried to focus deeper through my dragon—was that a thing?—but all I could tell was that the room I wanted was on the other side of a wall. I wandered toward the barrier, drumming my fingers on my legs. There had to be a way in that didn't involve melting walls.

An image flashed in my mind, and I reached for

it. A switch, behind a tile. Which one? The entire room was tiled in identical white squares. Which was creepy as fuck, but the longer I was conscious in this place, the more disconcerting all of it was.

I pressed my finger to a single spot, and pressed. Somewhere a latch clicked and a soft motor whirred.

Heat seared my thoughts, carrying a wave of images. Flame. Destruction.

"*Shield*," I shouted before I finished processing the images.

Fire roared around us, slamming into Magnus's invisible Valkyrie shield and not hitting us, but still searing my skin.

The ground rumbled under our feet, and the sound of explosions radiated out away from us. The doorway we came through was consumed by flame.

"We need to go." I was stating the obvious, and there was no time.

Frey shook his head. "We can't teleport. The walls—"

"Fuck." I let the possibilities tick through my mind, and turned to Artura. "Can we burn out the pieces of dragon in the walls?"

She nodded. "But the building will collapse."

Which was going to happen anyway. "Magnus, keep the shield up. Frey, be ready." No time for talk. For thought. They needed to obey. "Artura, we need to destroy the dragon fragments."

She frowned and closed her eyes.

I did the same, extending my senses through the building. Obliterating every piece I felt and cutting myself off from the structure more with each micro-destruction. If one person missed their cue, we'd be caught. In flame. In rubble. Very possibly between realms. The instant my connection to the building severed, I shouted, "*Now.*"

Flame and building chunks collapsed in on us as Magnus dropped her shield.

CHAPTER 27

FREYR

As Dahlia shouted *now*, my connection to the world returned. Magnus dropped her shield. I wrapped our group in a bubble of magic as fire singed us, and took us back to the apartment.

A collective gasp and sigh filled the room.

I was grateful Dahlia was all right.

I was more grateful Fen was all right.

A churn of emotions over what could have happened kept me reserved, holding back as I watched the rescue-mission-turned-battle once again turn into a reunion. Tension from a fight not-quite realized had my muscles and mind twisted in knots.

Dahlia sank into the seat nearest her. "I feel like I've just woken up from the worst sleep ever. I never want to sleep again, but I'm so tired."

"What happened?" As the adrenaline from the battle ebbed, I felt more myself. I sat next to her and rested a hand on her knee.

Dahlia scrubbed her face, a long sigh escaping through her fingers. As she explained the exchange with Minato, the betrayal and the nightmares, my anger surged back, but not at her.

"That's fucked up," Magnus said when Dahlia finished. "I forgive you for calling me a cunt."

Dahlia stuck her tongue out.

I was glad they could joke, but I had something more important to do. I extended my senses through the building, through everything NEON touched or was associated with, made sure my target wasn't already in any of those places, and adjusted the cloak that kept us safe. "Minato will never find this place again. It doesn't matter if she's standing right in front of the building, swearing it was right here."

"I think it's been a long day for all of us," Artura said. "Dahlia, I will help you learn, and you will take this exhausting mantle from me."

Dahlia wrinkled her nose. "You make it sound so appealing. But thank you."

"So, if you're leaving, can I get a lift?" Magnus asked. "You won't try to kill me again, now that you like Dahlia, right?"

Artura sighed. "Yes, and no."

"No you won't try to kill me, or no you don't like Dahlia?"

Artura settled a hand on Magnus's shoulder. "Have a good evening. I'll be in touch." They vanished from the room.

Fen knelt in front of Dahlia and I, taking each of our hands. "You want to sleep?"

"I really don't. Not until I'm too exhausted to think, and even then..." Dahlia frowned. "You shouldn't have come for me. I'm so fucking glad you did, but after everything..." She looked directly at me. "Especially you. Why?"

Because Fen wanted you back. That was the easy and obvious answer, but it wasn't the right one. I would have saved her solely because he asked me to, but that wasn't why. "You're a unique and brilliant and beautiful creature, and the world needs you. I want you around. I'll continue to do anything in my power to keep you from hurting Fen, but if you're not here, we can't continue to explore what you mean to us."

Her smile was tired, but it lit up her eyes. "You're going to let me stick around?"

"I'm going to *ask* you to spend more time here and hope you agree. Not only because you're my new opening act."

"When you put it that way... Okay. But can the dancing wait? I'm beat tonight."

"I've got something better in mind." We all needed to rinse the last several hours away. I stood and scooped her into my arms.

She wrapped her arms around my neck without protest and leaned into me. In the bathroom, I set her down on the plush rug next to the shower.

I pulled her shirt over her head, in a fluid movement. This wouldn't be fast and frantic; I wanted us to take our time. I kissed along her chest and shoulders while Fen unsnapped her bra and let it fall away, then dragged my mouth down her stomach and legs as I pushed her jeans and panties to the floor.

Fen lavished her neck and upper back with attention while I stripped off my clothes.

I turned on the shower and made sure the water was a few degrees on the right side of scorching while he undressed, then I grabbed Dahlia's hand and led her into the large tile and glass enclosure.

"Now, we pamper you," I said.

Her shy smile was so genuine, so unpracticed, it made me instantly hard. "Why?" she asked. "I've caused so much trouble. You had to rescue me like some fucking damsel in distress."

"You've had your mind torn out, rearranged, and played with too many times in your life. Today was the most recent, but I know it's not the only instance." My reply bounced in my thoughts as the words fell past my lips. What I told Artura earlier, that she was lucky Dahlia was the one stepping into this role, was truer than the ancient dragon could fathom.

Dahlia was so young, in the grand scheme of things. A human adult, but an immortal youngling. "You've already seen so much, been subject to so much, in your lifetime. You're resilient. You've bounced back and learned and grown, but that doesn't mean you always have to suck it up and just take it. Sometimes even the strongest of us deserve to be pampered."

"Well when you put it like that." She caught her bottom lip between her teeth.

Fen and I took our time lathering her body and ensuring we didn't miss a single inch of soft, supple skin. He lingered on her breasts, pinching and twisting her nipples, while I gave her pussy extra attention. Enough to draw her arousal out, but not enough to let her climax.

If being an old soul were a thing for the non-cursed individual, I would wonder how many lifetimes Dahlia had lived before this.

It didn't matter though, because she would live hundreds, maybe thousands, going forward.

CHAPTER 28

DAHLIA

Frey's words warmed me as much as his touch. I hated that I'd fought with him about Artura. That I still felt lost and tiny in this entire immortal scheme.

But as Fen worked the shampoo through my hair, taking his time to massage my scalp, I loved that I had these two incredible immortals watching my back.

Having a best friend who was a Valkyrie was great, Magnus would always be my sister, but Frey and Fen were different. I felt a closeness to them that Hel had always warned us not to fall into. That I never thought I'd live long enough to see.

I couldn't fathom eternity as a dragon, I frequently had a hard time seeing next week. But as Frey rinsed the soap from my body while Fen teased between my legs, I was confident that I'd like seeing how the chips landed. Figuring things out along the way would be fun.

Fen slipped his fingers inside me, and Frey stroked my clit. Their touches were light and playful, but my body was eager for the release. It didn't take much to coax me toward the peak and push me into orgasm. As I came, I ground into their hands, pressing for more and more until it was too much. I was glad they held me up as pleasure raked my body, even after they pulled their hands away.

We all rinsed each other off one more time, and stepped out of the shower. Frey rubbed and patted me dry with a towel.

Fen dried my hair, then planted both of us in front of a mirror. I watched our reflections with fascination as he drew a comb through my long black strands, then pulled the still damp locks into a braid.

The two of them, Frey and Fen, were so gorgeous. How had I captured their attention? I didn't want to question it too much, because it felt better to focus on how much I liked being with them.

The pampering was incredible, and I wanted to return the favor. I turned to Frey, head bowed, and looked up at him through my lashes. "Let me worship you." My request came out breathy.

He placed a finger under my chin and tilted my

head to meet my gaze. "Only because you asked so sweetly."

He led me into the bedroom, and Fen followed.

Frey lay back on the bed, looking every bit the stunning god he was.

I crawled up his body, my breasts brushing his legs and my ass in the air. When I glanced over my shoulder, I found Fen watching me with an alluring hunger. "I'm here to be taken." I wiggled my behind.

His grin showed a hint of fangs and my pulse screamed in response.

Returning my attention to my god of sex, I dragged my tongue up Frey's cock and licked along the head, relishing the low sounds rumbling from his chest. When I took him in my mouth, his groan raked over me like skilled fingers.

"Look at me," Frey commanded. "I want to watch you while you revere me."

An order I had no desire to refuse. I met his gaze. Could I drown in the heated blue that stared back at me?

I stroked and sucked, and his every response cranked my desire higher. Being pampered was nice, but offering myself at this alter was pretty fucking incredible too.

Fen slide the head of his cock along my slit, teasing forward to brush my clit, then gliding back to nudge one opening and then the other. I didn't take any of my attention from Frey, but I groaned and relished each stroke of Fen's teasing slip over my slick skin.

Fen slipped inside me, and I grunted at the penetration. He didn't move once he was buried to the hilt.

Frey thrust harder against my face, pumping with abandon. I relaxed my throat to let his full length slide in. Fen didn't move aside from the occasional twitch of his cock, until he reached forward to knead my breasts.

I sucked Frey with enthusiasm, loving his taste and feel in my mouth and the way he fucked my face harder when I stroked his balls.

This was different from any sex I'd had before. I could taste more. Fell more. Smell *more*. Fen's wolf was barely leashed, and the power flooding Frey was of a potency I struggled to fathom.

My own beast reveled in this moment, absorbing every sensation.

Frey gripped the base of my braid, holding my head in place. I could get lost in this rush of electricity and lust and physical need. I wanted to taste him. I needed to feel his release.

A salty spurt hit the back of my throat, his seed sliding down as he came hard. I sucked until he slowed to a stop, needing to experience all of this.

As I pulled away, I licked him clean with a just-rougher-than-normal tongue, and delight filled me at his shudder. My deceptively innocent look of *did I do that* vanished when Fen dug his fingers into my hips and began to pound inside me.

As he hit just the right spot with each thrust, pleasure surged through me. I was more turned on, more sloppy wet, than I'd realized. The way Frey watched us, his easy smile clouded with lust, amplified my arousal.

Fen reached around to stroke my clit. Was it too much? My body wasn't sure. He pushed past the uncomfortable numbness, never easing up the pace he hammered against me with.

Orgasm creeped up, toeing the edge but not letting me tumble over.

Fen adjusted his angle, and I fell into climax, losing track of myself as release flowed through me. As Fen spilled inside me. Stars danced behind my eyelids. Pleasure filled me from head to toe, and didn't fade even as Fen slowed to a stop.

We lay there for a while, I didn't know how long, before Fen left to clean up, and returned to help me do the same.

"I feel so spoiled," I teased.

Fen brushed his lips over mine. "Sometimes a woman deserves this kind of attention. You don't have to get used to it, but you should expect more of it."

Frey pulled me back into him, and Fen lay facing me.

He kissed the tip of my nose. "Next time they

come for you, they'll have to go through us," Fen said. "They should've had to this time."

I wanted to argue his certainty that TOM wasn't done with me, but he was right. Until TOM figured out how to destroy a dragon, or lock one away for eternity, they'd keep looking. I wish I understood why, but I didn't doubt that it would happen.

Frey draped a lazy arm over my hip. "That means no more running away."

"I won't apologize." I'd learned that from watching him. "Except for getting caught. Total noob move on my part." I swore I could hear Frey's eyeroll in his heavy sigh, and I didn't try to fight my smile. "What next?"

Fen raised my hand with his, palm to palm. Fur and claws appeared as his fingers elongated and he wove them through mine. "Can you do that?"

"Dragons don't have fur," I teased.

Frey slapped my ass lightly, and I giggled.

With a flicker of thought and will, I changed my own hand into one with scales and claws of its own. The dim light caught the occasional hint of violet and kept the hand visible in the dim light. "Apparently so."

"That's what's next," Fen said. "We help you learn more. Become more. And then we take this fight to TOM's door. Not just for you, but for everyone who's had to hide, or who's died, because they bought into a book full of *might happen*."

Frey drew his lips up the side of my neck. "No more running away."

"You figure things out with us." Fen kissed the back of my hand.

They were asking a lot more than it appeared—a kind of trust I didn't know if I had, but I was willing to try. They hadn't let me all the way in, and I understood why not. How did someone push past the centuries of adoration Frey and Fen had for each other, not to divide them, but to become a part of them?

If they were willing to have me around to find out if it was possible, I was more than happy to explore the same. "No more running away. I promise."

FREY STOOD next to me in the dressing room backstage at NEON, as I gave myself one last look in a full length mirror. The dress The Tailor made me was perfect—a simple white top and skirt that flowed together to look like Princess Leia's outfit from A New Hope, and as I tore each piece away, I'd expose the gold bikini underneath.

My hair was part of a dragon glamor—a long braid twisted on top of my head, secured under a tiara, and falling down my back. When I whipped my head with my dance, it would move with me.

Frey tugged the braid and met my reflection's gaze. "You look amazing."

"Thank you." I was both excited and nervous to be doing this. Dancing on stage because I wanted to. Because we'd created an amazing performance and I couldn't wait to share it.

He grasped my hand, spun me to face him, and kissed my fingertips. "I'll be watching. You'll be brilliant."

Warmth spread through me and I couldn't hide my grin. "See you when I'm done." I headed toward the stage.

Fen was waiting in the wings, and he grasped my wrist as I approached. He wrapped an arm around my waist, pulling me close.

I rested my palm on his chest, stopping him, but also using the beat of his heart to keep my nervousness at bay. "Careful of the makeup."

"Says the woman who can make her face look like anything." He dipped his head.

I stepped back with a laugh, breaking his grasp. "I can, but Frey spent a lot of time making me look perfect."

"I've got to say it. You always look perfect."

"You still can't kiss me until I'm done."

He tapped the tip of my nose. "Then go knock 'em dead, and get back here."

An upbeat tune resembling the Star Wars cantina music filled the club, and a smattering of excitement filtered from the main room. As the curtain came up, the noise grew to loud whistles and cheers.

I flowed into the dance, a series of kicks and hip swings and shimmies and so much more. This felt incredible. The movement. The attention. The freedom. I loved every minute of it.

When the music ended, I exited to more applause. Fen was waiting for me. He held out a robe, and when I reached for it, he pulled it back enough to threaten my balance.

He wrapped an arm around my waist, pulled me close, and kissed me hard. "I could watch that every night forever," he murmured against my lips.

"Forever is a long time." Yup. I loved every minute of this.

"I know that better than you do."

I laughed into another kiss.

The sound of Frey clearing his throat wasn't enough to interrupt us. Until he made the sound a second time.

Fen let me go, and we faced Frey.

My amusement vanished when I saw the woman standing next to him. She was as tall as Fen, with hauntingly pale skin and silver hair.

Frey's expression was flat. "Dahlia, this is—"

"Urd." I'd never met her, but I knew the instant my gaze locked with hers that she was the third dragon.

I stood in the apartment I'd been sharing with Dahlia for less than two months. The furnishings were sparse, but new. We were working on it. Beds had come first, of course. A couch, TV, and gaming consoles were next—it was all about the priorities.

It felt so empty here tonight. The kind of void that consumed part of me.

I shook the thought aside. Dahlia hadn't moved out; she was just spending more time at NEON than before. And she'd only gone there to begin with, at the start of all of this TOM hunting her stuff, because I was away doing other things with Kirby.

This was just one of those times I wasn't in the mood to be alone.

Nothing to do for it but eat an entire large pizza

by myself and play my favorite cart racer until I was so silly tired I was running into walls.

Someone knocked. Dinner was here. I checked the peephole, saw the back of the head covered with a cap from the pizza place, and opened the door.

The delivery guy spun and my stomach dropped into my shoes when I found myself face to face with Bragi. His hat hid shoulder-length blond hair that was probably braided the same way his beard was. Once upon a time I would've done *anything* he asked, and I'd fantasized more than once about him backing me against a wall and me begging him to fuck me.

Mostly because he was the one god I knew at TOM who I believed wouldn't do anything like that. Not without some intensely sexy consent.

That was once upon a time, though. Now, he was a little frightening, especially since this was the second time he'd shown up out of the blue in a place he shouldn't have found me.

I hid my muddled reaction to seeing him behind an eyeroll. "The hat doesn't do you justice."

"No? Shame." He yanked it off and stuffed it into the back pocket of his jeans. "Gave the guy a fifty for that plus the pizza." He handed me a large pizza box. "Dinner's on me, by the way."

"Not my pizza," I lied. The smell of the pepperoni made my stomach grumble.

"No? It's got your name on it." Bragi leaned

against the wall outside my apartment door, not making any attempt to coax his way in, balanced the box on one hand, and pulled out a slice with the other. The cheese was still so hot and melty it pulled in strings. He managed to close the lid with his elbow and take a bit of the food without disrupting the rest of the pie.

He took his time chewing and swallowing. "Whomever it was for, they're missing out."

I crossed my arms. "What do you want?"

"To say *hello*, catch up, and I was hoping share some pizza. You sure you don't want some?" He held out the slice.

It really did look good, and it was from my favorite place. An irrational temptation snaked inside to lean in and take a bite of his offered food. Instead, I grabbed the rest of the box from him. "Thanks. Enjoy your night." I swung the door shut.

It stopped short when it struck his foot. "Invite me in."

"What are you, a vampire?" Oh, fuck, vampires weren't real, were they?

Bragi set his half-eaten pizza on the top of the box I held. "Someone who wants to have this conversation in private."

"Too bad." I set my foot opposite his on the other side of the door. Just because he'd given us Dahlia's location didn't mean I trusted him. Who knew what kind of agenda he had?

"Fine. I'll stand on your landing and tell you. TOM will come for Dahlia again. When she was one of them, she created a piece of code more powerful than she fathomed. They've blended her tech with magic and use it to monitor a variety of incidents, like monitoring to see if anyone teleported from NEON. It was how they knew she was in Australia.

"They can't finish this merger of magic and tech without her, and now that they know what she is, that she can't be killed, they won't be gentle in subduing her. They'll come for you, and it will be the same. The two of you aren't safe anywhere."

Ice slid down my spine at his tone, and I masked the reaction. "Obviously, since you're here."

"I'm not your enemy, but no one can know that."

"Great. Thanks. Bye." I pushed the door, but it didn't budge.

Bragi reached past the pizza box—the only thing keeping us truly apart. He gripped my chin and pressed a pepperoni greased thumb to my bottom lip as he forced my gaze to his. "I don't want to see you hurt. Don't put me in that situation."

The door gave when he vanished, and I almost lost my balance.

I closed the apartment, flipped every lock into place, and slid to the ground, letting the pizza box drop to the floor in front of me. Maybe I wasn't okay with being alone tonight.

THANK you for reading the first book in Dahlia, Fen, and Frey's story. Things are calm now, but TOM is still a threat, and Dahlia has a lot to learn about being a dragon. To discover what happens next, check out CORRUPTION. How can Dahlia know who to trust when everyone around her is corrupt?